CLIMBING FURTHER UP VERITAS MOUNTAIN

One Man's Journey with the Lord

RYAN PAUL YOUNG

iUniverse, Inc.
Bloomington

Climbing Further Up Veritas Mountain
One Man's Journey with the Lord

iUniverse books may be ordered through booksellers or by contacting:

iUniverse
1663 Liberty Drive
Bloomington, IN 47403
www.iuniverse.com
1-800-Authors (1-800-288-4677)

ISBN: 978-1-4759-3694-0 (sc)
ISBN: 978-1-4759-3695-7 (ebk)

Printed in the United States of America

iUniverse rev. date: 07/18/2012

Contents

Dedication

THIS BOOK IS DEDICATED:

- To my parents for forming me in the Truth.
- To my wife for keeping me in the Truth.
- To my children: What is provided in this book is the most important message I can give you as your father: I love you all. I will see you at the finish line . . . .

PrePrologue

MANY HAVE ASKED WHY I am revising "Climbing Veritas Mountain." It is simply because I have learned more since I wrote the last book. I do not believe anything written in "Climbing Veritas Mountain" was wrong. The Lord has simply led me higher on the mountain of understanding.

The irony is that I am mostly re-discovering the Truths I have already been taught since as early as the third grade. For example, I learned from page one of the Baltimore Catechism that the meaning of life is to "know, love, and serve the Lord." After years in school, reading books, praying, debating, thinking, and questioning those at the highest levels of theological understanding and wisdom, I find that my conclusions are wrapping up where I started off . . . the third grade lesson to "know, love, and serve the Lord." I have simply come to a better understanding of "Why?"

Over the past year, the purpose of my being, my existence, has become abundantly clear to me. I have a singular mission: To invite as many eternal souls to the foot of the Cross that I possibly can, and to encourage those souls to die to themselves in order to allow the grace from that Cross to fill their lives.

Thank you in advance for walking with me up this stretch of my mountain. I hope this book serves as a tool to help you in the journey up your mountain to the foot of that same Cross. Prepare yourself for a fantastic adventure to peace and joy! Paradise with God in Heaven is worth every step!

Foreword

IT IS WITH TREMENDOUS HONOR that I take the opportunity to comment on the content of this book and the amazing man behind its words. Having known Ryan since the tender age of 18, I have had the pleasure of being by his side throughout his evolution into the man of God he is today. He is, among other things, a loving and steadfast husband, father and son, an evangelist, and a seeker of Truth and Justice. He has conquered many obstacles to become those things over the years and has been a hero to me with his unwavering devotion to discerning the Will of God in his life.

If there is one impression many people have after a conversation with Ryan, it is that he is passionate and dedicated to not only what he currently believes, but also to the search for something more: Truth. I have witnessed him spending his adult life in the pursuit of Wisdom and Justice, attempting to learn more about the God with whom he wants to spend the rest of his eternal life. His spiritual journey has consisted mainly of seeking, recognizing, internalizing, defending, teaching, and sharing little morsels of truth he has gathered throughout the years.

Collecting the tidbits set forth in this book about various subjects has been an adventure of sorts. Ryan would not consider himself a scholar, but he has been open to hearing and absorbing the advice and insights of all of those around him, likeminded or not. I have been with my husband for the formation of many of the thoughts in this book, whether derived from meditation, dinners with friends and family, consults with his patients, books, the Bible, the Catholic Catechism, or even movies. I can attest to the earnest process by which Ryan carefully and prayerfully separates out the truth in what he hears and reads. This book was not meant to be a textbook, but Ryan has painstakingly tried to ascertain the validity of his opinions prior to including them. If there are items that do not conform to the truths held within Catholic teaching, I can assure you that it is truly unintentional on his part.

Along the way, many of our friends and relatives have been instrumental in not only shaping and refining Ryan's thoughts, but also encouraging the propagation of these teachings through inviting him to speak to a large group or supporting him in the formation of a youth camp. Ryan has formed stores of appropriate stories and words of wisdom for various daily struggles and has been bold enough to share these when he encountered someone in need of comfort or help finding God. The process began many, many years ago of starting to record the stories mainly so he would not forget them. This book has now evolved into a record of these insights; however, it began as simply a way for a loving father to share his journey with the Lord for the sake of his children. As a father, he wants only that his children have eternal life with God. His secondary desire is for his children to know him, love him and want to be with him forever, much as Ryan's only life's goal has become to know God, love God, and be with Him forever in Heaven.

Ryan firmly believes that we are in a war for souls. In writing this book, he hopes to arm his children with a shield of self-awareness and a sword of Truth. I could not be more proud of the man Ryan has become, and in many ways has always been. He is a true inspiration to me, our family, our friends and our community and I am not ashamed to say that I consider myself the luckiest woman alive to be at his side in his journey to Christ. Enjoy this book as I have enjoyed immensely the many nights we have labored together over the formation of its contents.

Forever in Christ,

Elizabeth Young

Prologue

I AM NOT AN AUTHOR. I am not even a decent writer. I have never in my wildest imagination ever contemplated that I would be sitting down at this moment, writing to you. I have no real expectation that a single soul will ever read this book. I must die to *my* will.

I am on a journey. This journey is a walk with the Lord where my only task is to let Him lead the way. This journey has thus far taken me in directions I didn't know were possible for me. He has requested of me things I did not think I could do. I have no knowledge of where the Lord will take me in this life. I must die to *my* will.

This conversation with you is the next step in my walk with the Lord. For some reason, the Lord has requested me to write down little bits of wisdom I have learned so far in my short life. I don't fully understand the Lord's reasoning in this venture. After all, I am a very weak man, sinful in thought and deed. The only power I have is to choose to obey God or not. I must die to *my* will.

Throughout my whole life I have wanted to be in control. I wanted to know and to ensure that I would be "successful" in everything I did. I found that I had a skewed worldly perception of "success." I measured success in dollars, influence, power, praise, and control of others. I formerly would have questioned myself at this moment, asking "why am I taking the time to write a book that I do not know a soul on this earth will actually publish, much less read?" I asked myself this before giving up my time because I didn't want to give up control over my most precious commodity, my time. A constant struggle within me is restraining *my* will. I must repeatedly shut down my instinct to control, rooted in Original Sin, and try to live a life where I die to *my* will.

If I can give up my control, if I can die to my will, I can truly be free from failure and worry because in a spiritual sense, there is **no such thing as failure in *attempting* to do the will of the Lord.** The Lord does not guarantee "success" as I would have formerly defined it. I believe He does guarantee peace and joy and ultimately eternal salvation for those who allow Him to control the path of their life. The reality is that worldly success no longer matters as much to me because in dying to myself, in dying to *my* will, and replacing my will with the will of the Lord, I feel I have already eternally succeeded.

Again, I do not fully understand why the Lord has requested that I write down some of the Truth He has shared with me. I am not even fully clear about how I learned much of what I will share with you. I do know that if you are reading this book, **it is not by accident.** Hopefully one of the lessons the Lord has taught me in my life may be applicable to you.

I pray at this moment that I have the courage to write what the Lord intends. I pray that those reading this can dive into the arms of the Lord as would an innocent trusting child, finding peace, joy, and eternal bliss. I pray that I can die to *my* will . . . .

Ryan Paul Young

THE MEANING OF LIFE

Tick, tock, tick, tock, tick, tock . . . time. I started to think a lot about time when I was just beginning high school. Time was passing and passing by quickly and I didn't have a point to my life. I found myself locked in a routine. We all know about routines. Mine consisted of waking up before sunrise to the obnoxious beeping of my alarm clock, showering in cold water (I was always competing for hot water with my six sisters), eating nearly the same thing every day for breakfast and lunch, waiting for the bus, going to class, working after school, watching TV, talking to friends and then repeating the same pointless routine, day after day after day. Why, I finally asked? Was there anything that I was doing with my time on a daily basis that was actually going to last? Is there more to life than whether the Jets win on Sunday or who in Hollywood is cheating with whom? The interests of the world seemed so shallow. At the end of my days I knew I would die. I knew that we all have a 100% mortality rate, the question is simply when. Whether I liked it or not, this was a hard, cold fact. Why bother with the effort of life if it would all end anyway? Why spend all my time doing what the world expected me to do? Without a reason to my life, I was living a life without peace and joy. I felt so empty.

Before having purpose and meaning to my life, I had moments of "happiness." I would feel happy when I felt "full" emotionally, physically, and mentally. The problem with my life and my actions at that time was that the happiness that I experienced was fleeting and brief. I was always looking for the next big fix, which might be experienced with one more vacation, one more material good, one more girlfriend, one more achieved earthly success. I was never able to sustain that feeling of "happiness" and would always return to that inner void of emptiness. What I really sought was meaning and purpose to my life.

I call it the "Superbowl syndrome." Imagine a professional athlete practicing football his whole life and finally making the NFL. After years in the NFL, he finally makes it on a team that wins a lot of games. He gives it his all throughout the season, diving and fighting for the ball. He finally makes it to the Superbowl and his team wins. He experiences absolute jubilation and 'happiness' for about five minutes. He then asks himself, "now what?" I had to reevaluate. What were my 'Superbowl' ambitions? Were my objectives *lasting* objectives?

When I was in high school, I would set a goal for myself like getting an 'A' on a test or win a championship in sports. I would study or play hard and yes, (even a blind squirrel finds a nut every once in a while), at times I would actually stumble upon the 'A' or trophy I sought. My motivation at the time was completely about self. I was getting the 'A' to receive praise from my parents and peers, as well as to make a lot of money one day. I worked on earning trophies so I could impress the young ladies at school. At the time, **nearly every motivation of every act I did was to build self.** Every act I did was to earn gains in earthly sex, money, and power. I wanted control.

Since then I have observed thousands of people, of all ages, wandering through life the way I did in high school. I used to work in New York City and commute every day on the train. People in suits would be holding the same kind of coffee in one hand, with the same newspaper in the other, and would know the exact spot where the train door would open once it would finally arrive. They would enter the train and sit in the same seat they always used, turn to their left and say "Good morning Fred," then to their right and say "Good morning Susie." It is not that I perceive routine as evil. Rather it is routine without purpose and meaning that kills our spiritual being. It was like a "rat race" where the rat wasn't even really in a race but was running on a treadmill and going nowhere. It was on this commute that I thought about how far the Lord had taken me up to that point in time. I realized with joy that I had been spared becoming a machine. In finding purpose, I jumped off of the conveyer belt of pointless routine. I had been spared spiritual emptiness.

I was able to avoid that fate because I stopped to ask the question: Why? Why are we here? What is the point of life? I believe all humans have asked these questions consciously or subconsciously at some time during their life. There seems to be some kind of magnet in our human chemistry that draws us to seek the Truth in this regard.

The first question I think we must all address is as follows: Is there is a God? If I were to see a piece of trash, such as a cardboard box, lying on the sidewalk, would I think that the box existed by mere chance? Would I truly believe that different organic material such as trees spontaneously broke down into an evolutionary cycle of organic soup and through millions of years formed itself into a cardboard box? Or would I just think to myself, "WHO put the cardboard box in the middle of the sidewalk?" As simple as a box is, I would logically assume that someone made and designed that box. Similarly, I can't look at a human being without awe knowing the complexity of our design. Logically, there has to be a designer. After all, am I not more complicated than a cardboard box?

Thinking of it a different way; is it realistic to imagine a tornado blowing through a junkyard and, through chance alone, create a 747 airliner with all of the working circuit boards and capacity to fly? I don't look at an airplane and think to myself, "Boy, the Big Bang really did a terrific job in creating that aircraft." Logically, I would have some common sense and faith that this 747 must be the design of some engineer. I would marvel at the engineer that could create such an amazing thing. Am I not more complex than a 747 airplane?

Listening to premier scientist's incredibly creative (and often ridiculous) hypotheses on how we could possibly exist without a God always seems to ultimately give me more faith in the simple Truth that there is a God. These scientists lengthy guesswork about events that happened billions of years ago stretches the imagination so far that I am curious if any one of them truly believes in *his own* explanation. We struggle to figure out how the Egyptians had such a functional civilization 6 thousand years ago (in many ways more functional than 75% of the civilizations in the world today) and yet this same guy is going to try to convince me of what he thinks happened hundreds of billions of years ago? . . . Yeah . . . The reality is that with every guess a scientist puts forth in how we could have possibly come to existence without the existence of God, that does not mean that is how it *actually* happened. In Truth, no one really has any idea. Science answers the question of *What* something is. Science still struggles with the questions of *How* and *Why?*

Human beings are not only built with created matter which allows us to function and move, but we have also been built with life. We are not just a rock or some gas. We have the capacity to think, love, communicate, dream, laugh, cry, empathize, hope, forgive, create, and feel. You can't get these abilities in a rock or atom or molecule independently. There must be a creator.

The fact that we were designed so well is amazing but our *maintained* existence is also a miracle in and of itself. In my professional life, I work in the field of medicine. It is surprising to see how easy it is to die. It is incredible how many parts have to work perfectly for us to be able to live. If one organ system is not perfect, we die. The fact that our heart beats without our effort 60-100 beats per minute and if it stops for several minutes we die; *that* is a miracle. The fact that we go through our entire lives able to breathe air and if we were to stop breathing for several minutes we die; *that* is a miracle. Think about how little you have to do with your body's existence right now as you read this book. Your heart is beating, you are breathing, and you have numerous temperature and blood pressure regulators working. What effort are you expending in this process? Our body's capacity to repair cells automatically when we heal is also a miracle. Knowing what I know about the human body and about what can go wrong with our bodies, I can't believe we can actually live to be 100 years of age.

The whole notion that we can exist without God, our designer and engineer, is rather absurd to me. It simply does not follow several basic rules of "science." The first such scientific rule is that something cannot come from nothing. Even with the argument that the matter in the "big bang" could have existed forever (which I don't believe), it still does not explain how the matter of the universe spontaneously and accidentally could create life. Finally, it does not explain how that life form can possess the ability to think and love. Yes, the prior points are 3 independent **nearly impossible,** and in the very least, extremely implausible 'scientific' scenarios that would clearly need a creator.

Professionally, I am also a scientist of sorts. I think the world mistakenly perceives that science is the attempt to disprove the existence of God. I believe that **science is the study *of* the creation of God.** As I look at science in that light, it completely enhances my knowledge of God and Creation and consequently, my relationship with God deepens even further. I am able to marvel at His grandeur in space, the environment, and our bodies.

I am not alone in this view of science. Many scientists initially set out to disprove God and then discovered in their scientific pursuit that the mathematical possibility of us existing without Him is essentially impossible. I would argue that an Atheist requires far more "faith" in the impossible than one who acknowledges the existence of God.

What about evolution? I don't think it matters. Evolution does not disprove God. You would still need God to create something before that something could evolve. You would still need order and oversight to keep life in existence. If God created the universe and that universe evolved with God's oversight, who cares whether or not evolution exists? The Truth is He created us either way.

After we conclude that God must exist, I still questioned, "why me?" Why did He create me? Why give us this life? In my observation of people, I came to a startling realization: we have been *given* everything that identifies us. We were born into our bodies, our looks, talents, family, country, wealth, station, everything. We had no control over any of these things at birth. We have limited control over these realities even as we get older. Whether you were born predisposed to being rich, poor, fat, skinny, ugly, gorgeous, psychologically imbalanced, intelligent, or any combination thereof, we all have only one thing in common from birth: *our free will.* **The only common attribute of all human beings is the ability to choose, moment to moment, what we are going to do with the station, talents, looks, intelligence, wealth, and so forth that we have been given.** This Truth brought me to understand the meaning of life. **THE MEANING OF LIFE IS TO CHOOSE ETERNITY WITH GOD!!!!**

We have been given this split second, this blink of eternity's eye, to make a choice. Again, I found that if I believe in God and understand that my only possession is my free will, what else could this life be for?

Think about it for a minute; if you loved someone, would you force them to be with you for eternity? If you were a parent and you shackled your kids to the floor of your basement for eternity stating "I will force you to be with me and you must love me," *is that love?* **Can there be love or relationship without the freedom to choose it?** If God created us without choice and chained us to Heaven's wall, could you call that love or would it become slavery?

In order for us to have the capacity to love, we must have the choice of not loving. Love itself cannot exist without a free-will. Once I understood that my purpose in life is this decision to choose relationship with Him, to choose Love, everything came into focus. Now there is a reason for my existence. Now there is a purpose to every breath I take on a daily basis. Now there is a reason for every action and decision I make. Life has become a lot more meaningful.

Once I found that Heaven is my objective, my entire "priority list of life" changed. **What is more important than Heaven?!!** My relationship with God and His mission for me now takes precedence over all my former "worldly" goals. If I am the most "successful" individual in every earthly way, including family, money, power, education, and earthly influence, and then die and have not chosen relationship with God, my entire life has been an utter waste. If I do not choose Heaven, I truly would have lived a meaningless life and would have wasted the very point of my existence. Without choosing relationship with God, I could not be further from the Truth and Reality of my creation, **in fact I would have just wasted the very essence of everything I was built to be.**

Now, the priority of my life is to strive for eternity with God. That priority influences every decision I make. This influenced which college I attended, who I decided to marry, what major I chose in college, my political affiliation, my identity . . . everything. There is no decision on earth that would warrant ignoring the objective of Heaven and avoiding my relationship with God.

In understanding the meaning of life, I now experience joy. The difference between the happiness I would formerly experience in reaching my worldly goals, and joy, is that *joy lasts.* I perpetually feel good at my emotional baseline. I feel other emotions like sadness, anger, jealousy, happiness, ambition, inadequacy, and so forth, but at my baseline, I always return to joy. I have peace. I know where I came from and where I am going. My daily routine now has purpose. I am no longer just "going through the motions of life." The journey of life has become so much easier that I feel like I am walking downhill.

Not everyone in the world has *worldly* freedom. Some people are born into tyranny. However, with a free will, we can all have *spiritual* freedom. We have the freedom to use our free will in every situation, good or bad, and we have the freedom to use our free will to choose relationship with God . . . or not.

Please don't think I am saying that if you understand the meaning of your life, you will not suffer. The truth is quite different. The truth is that even while suffering—if you and I understand that in every moment of every day we have an opportunity to choose God—we can be joyful in that suffering. This was shown by the first Christian martyrs as they were burned alive or fed to lions in the Coliseum. They were joyful and singing at their deaths. The point is this: **if you constantly choose relationship with God, in good situations and bad, you will have peace and joy at all times.** Lord, thank you for giving me purpose. Lord, thank you for drawing me to you. It was when I realized the true meaning of my life that my adventure with the Lord began.

CHOICE

IT IS 8:23 AM IN BAGHDAD, Iraq. This day, my mission and the fulfillment and culmination of my life will reach its apex. Thirteen minutes left. I am excited and anxious at this moment. I can feel sweat dripping down my back and covering my forehead under my turban. I don't know if I am sweating because of the stifling heat? I don't know if it's from the weight of the fiery deliverance buckled around my waist? I don't know if it's from fear? I am so petrified that I can taste bile in my mouth. Regardless, the harem that awaits me in heaven as promised by my earthly spiritual teacher, Mohammed Al Jahiff, is worth a bit of sweat and fear. I finally received the call by cell phone last night. I have prepared my whole life for this moment at my madrasa and I will not fail. These American infidels and Iraqi police, these traitors of Islam are about to know Allah's wrath! I feel honored that I can play a role in this holy Jihad. Here comes my target. These guys have no idea about what is about to hit them. It is time to reach for the trigger. Three, two, one, Praise ALLAH! . . . . BOOM!

This teenage Islamic male just died believing he was choosing God. Was he? How do we know? What is our standard for that perfect choice? Many will read that story and start a mental series of justifications for why they don't believe in "organized religion." They convince themselves to suspend the search for Truth altogether, and continue to *go out of their way* to avoid God as much as possible. They will choose to live life without meaning or purpose, choosing a finite life of emptiness and ignorance and will ignore the bigger picture of their existence. (Go Jets!!) Often, this is acted out with public displays of false humility with statements like, "How can anyone even begin to try to know or understand anything about something as great as God" . . .

Some completely discount all the knowledge and wisdom of everybody throughout the history of the world who have asked the same questions and who have often received sound answers in Truth through reason. Those who simply dump "organized religion," instead of standing on the shoulders of theological giants, start again to "create the wheel" on their own. Is this a wise course of action? Is it wise to believe that no one else throughout the history of our planet has ever had a thought in philosophy or theology that was a pretty good idea? It would be as foolish as trying to invent a computer from scratch now without first looking at and taking apart computers that presently exist. Nobody would rationally ignore the experiences of others regarding worldly experience and questions, why would ignoring the experience of others make sense regarding religious questions? Why does it seem so natural to ask advice about which car to buy, what to name your child, which doctor to see about your allergies, what school to attend and which outfit to wear to a certain event, but not seek or accept advice about our spiritual health? Why does it seem taboo to openly discuss what others believe and why? In reality, most of these "intellectuals" are just spiritually insecure or theologically lazy or they just do not want to acknowledge the Truth that there is a God, *and it is not them.*

What is ironic about this avoidance of God is that these same intellectuals generally affirm that they believe in the concept of good and evil. They would generally acknowledge a difference between the actions and beliefs of Hitler and Mother Theresa. They generally agree that the concepts of the Ten Commandments and charity and so forth are "good acts." If one believes in good and evil, inherently they must also believe in God because otherwise "good" would not be defined by anything and there would be chaos. **Without God, there is no order. Without God, there is no Truth. Without God, there is no difference between Hitler and Mother Theresa. Without God, we are just blobs of matter passing through the universe without point. Without God,** *there is no such thing as good and evil. What do you believe?*

I do not believe, as Agnostics do, that God would create us and give us a free will to then abandon us to live lives without purpose or meaning. God gave us the perfect standard. He gave us "the Way, the Truth, and the Life."(Jn 14:16) He gave us *Himself* as Jesus Christ. Who would be a better example of perfection than God Himself? No longer is the choice for God ambiguous. No longer is Truth some vague, gray, abstract, unattainable idea. In the Incarnation of God into the man of Jesus Christ, no longer is God some being out in space that is completely out of touch with Humanity. Through the life of Jesus Christ, Reality in Truth for the perfection of our will walked the very Earth in which we now live. He breathed the same air. In His humanity, He was tempted and suffered yet He still lived perfection, as He was God.

This Good News of the Incarnation, God becoming man, was shouted in praise from the Heavens both at the Annunciation (When the Archangel Gabriel revealed to Mary that she would bear the savior of the world) and from legions of angels at Christmas to the shepherds "And suddenly there was a multitude of the heavenly hosts with the angel, praising God and saying: "Glory to God in the highest and on Earth peace to those on whom him favor rests."(Lk 2:13).

Why Jesus? Why not Mohammed, or John Smith, or Buddha and so forth? I ultimately had to ask myself this question, "If I were to choose from all the prophets and holy men throughout time to be my savior, my 'perfect example and choice,' who would it be?" If the meaning of life is to choose God, I have yet to find another religion where God *Himself* came to Earth to be the "Perfect Choice" and ultimately redeem mankind. Other religions have a "great prophet," but they don't claim to have God Himself as their standard.

The most basic moral standard of our country and most the world is generally, "love your neighbor as yourself." The world's basic moral standard (Natural Law) follows the teaching of Jesus, whether the world knows this or not. There is no individual throughout all of time that has more dramatically changed the world's view of morality than Jesus Christ. I would love to tell you every detail I know about His life at this moment, but I would not have enough pages in this book to do so. If you are reading this book and do not know about the life of Jesus Christ, I implore you to read the Gospels in the New Testament or even watch the movie "Jesus of Nazareth," (1977), which may be cinematically outdated, but is a solid and scripturally based movie about the life of Jesus. Once you do that, you will then have to make a decision identified accurately by C.S. Lewis in "Mere Christianity." That decision is as follows: either

Jesus is a complete lunatic because He claims to be the Son of Man (God Himself), or Jesus Christ is who He claims He is. How could He be considered a "great prophet" or "nice historical figure" if He was a lunatic and a liar? *Which do you believe?*

If you have a general knowledge of the life of Christ and you are not sure whether He is a lunatic and a liar or that Christ is truly the Son of God, I ask you to consider performing a simple spiritual exercise. Find a large crucifix. Staring at Jesus on the cross, I want you to repeat out loud ten times, "Jesus, you are a lunatic, a liar, and a fraud. You did not die on that cross for me." In performing this exercise, it will force most to get off "the fence" and make a decision. If you can make it through that statement ten times and mean it, the rest of this book will likely not be very relevant to you.

Evidence of Christ's divinity was demonstrated by the stories documented throughout the New Testament. His divine life was outlined before Christ's birth through prophecy and revelation throughout the entire Old Testament. It was seen at His birth as Herod was willing to kill all male children less than two years of age in Christ's hometown of Bethlehem to prevent Christ from maturing. Again, even His enemies had faith in who He was. It was seen by three foreign Kings coming to pay Him homage. This was seen through His miracles that were acknowledged by both His friends *and* His enemies. This was proven most as he rose from the dead following his crucifixion. Christ's message fulfills the longing for Truth in every human heart. Christ's divinity is confirmed when all of his apostles except John were tortured to death and martyred for their faith. For the sake of argument, if they were just making this whole thing up, why were they willing to die horrible deaths for a hoax or a lie?

If you are with me up to this point and believe that God created us, gave us a free will to choose Him, and that Jesus Christ is the Truth, the Perfect Choice, then welcome to Christianity! Accepting the Bible as an authority for Truth *only then* makes sense. The entire Old Testament points to the coming of the Messiah. It is incredible that the lessons of the Old Testament and spiritual struggles of mankind thousands of years before the birth of Christ are the same battles we fight today. The Truth in Scripture stands out for this reason. Its Truth transcends time. The entire Old Testament ultimately provides only a shadow of God and His Will for us. Through the Old Testament God communicates through signs and wonders and prophets. It is only in the New Testament where the shadow of God is lifted by God Himself through becoming directly present to His people in the person of Christ Jesus. God has made it clear that if we can emulate Christ and follow His teaching, we will make the "perfect choice." We will be making the choice of Heaven as our ultimate objective.

Christ was Jewish and accepted the laws of the Old Testament for Himself. This validates the Truths set forth in the Old Testament. I don't believe the Son of God would follow the Old Testament unless the principles were true. The New Testament describes Christ Himself through the Gospels and the Apostles' accounts of their direct witness of Him. Again, logically, if Christ is the Messiah, the New Testament can be considered as True and inspired by God. It would not make sense for the God of the universe to become man to reveal to us the "Way, Truth and Life" only to die for our sins and not leave us any Truth of His teaching for mankind. It is therefore logical to believe that if Christ is the Messiah and the accounts of His life were inspired by God, the New Testament is also a valid "authority" in Truth.

If Christ is the Way, the Truth, and the Life, there is no further prophet needed to relay the wishes of God. Who can better offer us Truth than God Himself? That is why other religious texts, such as the Koran or the Book of Mormon that were written well after the life of Christ, are not necessary in the search for Truth. Christ didn't say "I am *mostly* the Truth and some other prophet will need to come after my time and finish the job . . ." As far as I know, neither those of Islam nor Mormons believe that Christ is a lunatic or a liar. The reasoning for the need of the teaching of Mohammed or John Smith is therefore unclear to me. That being said, many Muslims and Mormons, through their inherent desire to be good, whether they know it or not, *live* the life of Christ better than some Christians whose actions do not support what they supposedly believe. Who then, is making a better "choice" for God? Who then has a better relationship with God? Who then would most likely rest in His arms as would a child for eternity?

In my walk with the Lord, the awareness of these realities started to bring focus to my mission. That mission is to know Christ and to follow Christ as his disciple. The Truth sets me free of the worldly illusion to aspire for a meaningless, superficial life. In following Christ, I am free from the mental and spiritual programming of our society and culture. I am no longer deceived that the lie that sex, money, and power will bring me lasting joy. In many ways, by following Christ, I have experienced a taste of Heaven here on Earth. By acknowledging the Truth of Christ, I now have a spiritual focus and can live in the Truth with the *confidence* of knowing right from wrong, good from evil. I can be confident about the impact of my behavior. I now have a goal of perfection that I can attempt to reach. I now have lasting peace in the confidence that I am choosing Truth, thus I am choosing relationship with God, and will ultimately be in His arms for eternity in paradise. Jesus truly is the Way, the Truth, and the Life!

THE RELIGION OF SELF

I RECENTLY ATTENDED A MASS in upstate New York, and noted that the church was hardly attended. Those who were present were old. The priest, who was covering numerous parishes on his own, was old. There is only one shared Mass per weekend. Other than my family, there was no one in attendance under the age of 60. There was not even an organist. For one who absolutely loves the Church, it was like standing at the bedside of a family member that you deeply love that is terminally ill from a preventable disease. There is a feeling of helplessness. There is a sense of "How did we come to this?" The Catholic Church in that region will likely not exist ten years from now. I have attended many churches throughout the Northeast and noticed similar situations. The Catholic Church, as we know it, is dying in that area of our country.

It reminds me of my college semester abroad in Europe. I went into these fantastic, immense cathedrals throughout France, Germany, Hungary, and the Czech Republic, only to find the cathedrals nearly empty for Mass. It was like walking into a cold, dark tomb. These massive buildings were corpses of the life that once lived within them. That life was the Church, the community of believers who once worshipped together in unison as one body. This Church, this community of people cared for one another and was connected to the lives of the other members of that body. This community shared in each family's high points, such as a baptism and first communion, and would also be there for a family's low points, such as providing help when needed or being present to lend support during the death of one of its members. The church was a spiritual family then.

One afternoon I was talking to one of my childhood best friends. We were reflecting on the condition of the Catholic Church in today's society. I was very sad at the prospect of such goodness in our Church seemingly dying in my sight. He said something very profound. He noted that we now live in a society of individualism where the very concept of community and family is under full attack. With the family community under attack, the attack on the larger church community of the faithful would reasonably follow. In short, **the Church is ill because the family is ill. Why? Because the Church is family. The Church is relationship.**

This made a lot of sense to me. We now live in the age of "Seinfeld." I love watching that show. Occasionally, I still capture the episodes on my DVR. I find the program quite humorous. However, what disturbs me is that many of my friends and peers are actually living lives like those portrayed on that show. On the program you see four people living individual lives without a serious *commitment* to anything or anybody. They are gods unto themselves. There is never a moment when any one of them would *sacrifice* anything for anybody else. They simply live an amoral life, finding the next "fix" of happiness with their next meal, date, or entertainment prospect. Every moment of every day, their goal is to satisfy every animalistic desire . . . to feel emotionally full for a few moments. Every moment of every day is used to satisfy *self*. This drive to satisfy their emotional hunger is at any cost, regardless of the damage done to themselves, others, or the community at large. In the end there is nothing but absolute emptiness and loneliness. **In the end, there is nothing but *self*.** Instead of watching this TV series as an entertaining fictional story and satire of our culture, the "Seinfeld lifestyle" has now become the cultural "norm."

Growing up, the world promoted self above all else. I spent much of my youth preparing for the day when I would finally meet my spouse; the woman I had been praying for and about for years before I actually met her. Although I did not believe in this kind of thing at the time, when I finally met her at the age of 18 at an ice cream social the second day of college, I knew my life was hers. There was a kind of recognition, like remembering a dream. I finally met my other half; my "bone of my bones and flesh of my flesh," (Gen 2:23) my Eve. It was this moment after mere seconds of conversation that I told my older brother Robert, "I have found my wife." He logically looked at me skeptically and stated,

"Buddy, there are many great fish in this larger pond of college, slow down little brother." Regardless of his advice, I simply knew. I don't know how, I just knew she was me. The first Thanksgiving of freshman year of college, I slapped down her picture on the Thanksgiving table in front of my eight brothers and sisters and parents declaring that this shall be my wife! After rolling their eyes, they asked if I was even dating her yet. I confidently exclaimed "that she had a serious boyfriend that she thought she was going to marry," but I wasn't too worried about that . . . We did not even start dating till the following summer. We were engaged the summer after and I proposed to marry her following our third year in college. Little did I know the kind of backlash I was about to face!

When I decided to ask my wife to marry me, I cannot tell you how many people advised me to wait until I "established myself" before I got married. In essence, I was told to live this "Religion of self," this "Religion of Individualism" before giving myself up to the *commitment* of family. In the "Religion of Self," *my* needs were to come first. If it feels good, do it. In the "Religion of self," *I* am in control. In this religion, *I* am god. *My* education, my power was to come first. *My* career and money were to come first. There was nothing more important than *my* immediate pleasure, *my* quest for sex, so I should live a life that pretends I am married while living with a girlfriend, but without the commitment. Why avoid commitment one might ask? So I can easily *leave* the day any remote sacrifice is needed of me. This is the teaching of the world! Self, self, self, self, self!!! **There is nothing more threatening to the "Religion of Self" than the giving of self in marriage! There is *absolutely* nothing more threatening to the "Religion of Self" than the *sacrificial love* involved in bearing children!!** The "Religion of Self" is why abortion is viewed as 'necessary' today. The root of every abortion is self. The "Religion of Self" is why most are choosing to delay getting marriage till their late twenties and thirties. The "Religion of Self" is why there is a 50% divorce rate. Wake up brothers and sisters! "The Religion of Self" has taken a serious foothold over our culture!

My answer to the world was that I *knew* this woman was my wife. If I still needed more education, we would experience that together. If I was to be poor, and believe me, we were really poor (the entire belongings of both of us combined fit into a sedan. We literally sat on the floor of our first apartment and used our igloo cooler as our table), at least we would be poor *together in marriage*. We could not even afford a toilet paper holder for the first 3 years of marriage. Yes, you heard me right, a $10 toilet paper holder! If we were going to be poor separately, we might as well be poor together.

My point has been and still is that I will love her in good times and bad, in sickness and in health, for richer or poorer, till death we part. That was my oath to her. That remains my oath and my covenant to her this very day. **There is nothing to say what tomorrow will bring.** What is our oath/covenant worth? Does commitment mean anything? Do we understand that there is **no such thing as love without *sacrifice*?!! Denial and ultimately death to self is the path of real, lasting love.** This statement is anathema to the "Religion of Self." In the "Religion of Self," one can only sacrifice and live for *self*.

The "Religion of Self" has bled into the thought process of our entire culture. Our latest government "stimulus bill" is one more symptom of this "Religion of Self." We used to live in a country where we worked hard in order to provide our children with a future *better* than our own. No longer. We now "borrow" money from our children to get every 'entitlement' we can drown ourselves in today. Imagine at your parent's death, they left you a $200,000 bill that you had to pay now. That is the situation in which we are leaving our children. We are totally selfish.

Through our desire to control everything and be our own gods, the family unit and the essence of community is under attack. The fabric of our society, which is the family, is 'thread bare." The family is like an orchestra with many parts that, when working in unison, creates a symphony. If everyone in the family is living the "Religion of Self" and plays his own tune, the resulting music will sound disastrous. The family is the building block of all society. If society does not have a solid base in the family, all aspects of that society will suffer and ultimately collapse. Think about how many problems are rampant in our society today due to the lack of a strong family unit. Think about how many families no longer have a matriarch and a patriarch. The fight for control and power in our lives through the attempt to build self, is causing divorce and fornication and selfishness to become our cultural "norm." **In this** modern era of self, are we truly better off? Do more people have lasting joy in their lives?

The Church is a family. The Church is a community. The Church is relationship. The Church is referred to as "The body of Christ."(1Cor12:12) The Church is the antithesis of the "Religion of Self!"

In the "church" of my home, my family helps keep me grounded. My precious wife Elizabeth keeps my eyes focused on the "finish line" of Heaven. How often I am tempted to live only for myself. We gave ourselves to each other, totally and completely, in the holy sacrament of Matrimony. I have truly come to understand the statement that "two come together and make one flesh."(Mt 19:5) She is me. I am her. We are inseparable. It is somewhat unbelievable how well she truly knows everything about me. The greatest aspect of our relationship is that, in fully giving of ourselves to each other, we experience unconditional love. With that level of love, I have no fear. I am free knowing that as long as I draw breath, she will be committed to me and I her. There is nothing I can do or she could do that would jeopardize that reality. This allows complete honesty in our relationship.

I work hard. As an introvert, my daily interaction with people draws energy from me. Therefore when I return home, I am usually totally exhausted. It is that moment when I first enter the door that my children descend on me like a bunch of vultures to a carcass. As I walk through my house with children hanging from all of my appendages, I am so tempted to hide in a room and close the door for a while to recover.

It is these moments where Elizabeth calls me on to be better than I would be on my own. This time with my kids, hearing about their lives, is the most important thing I do on any given day. Although I would rather hide, they need me. When I battle the demons in my life, especially with the "Religion of Self," she draws me back, she draws me home. She reminds me about the meaning of my life. She reminds me about our community at home and about my responsibility within that "body." She reminds me about my priorities in the big picture. My soul is hers to tend to, and boy, considering how much of a screw up I am, the tending my soul is a testament to her sainthood. Miraculously, she might just get me to the finish line. In my commitment to her and to my family, I am fulfilling my vocation. I am doing what God intends for me to do. I have reason and purpose in my life. By fulfilling my commitment to my family, my church community, and my God, I am at peace. I am experiencing the Kingdom of God *right now*.

Our family community is a microcosm of the larger family, our Church. Ideally, we *could* give of ourselves, totally and completely to each other, experiencing unconditional love with everybody, all the time. In doing this, we would truly be making the "perfect choice" as set forth by Christ. In giving up the "Religion of Self," in giving up our control, we become truly free. True relationships and community *can be* experienced. The church in our region would then thrive as its members would experience peace and joy. Again, this possibility can happen only if the family cell is repaired and healed. How can we repair the community of the Church if our "church" at home is in disrepair? How can we repair relationships within the "Body of Christ" at church if we have not repaired our relationships at home?

By identifying the enemy as the "Religion of Self," we now can take active steps in avoiding its downfall. Become aware of how we are being programmed through our public education and media. Resist becoming the "army of one." Give up control to God, **die to self**, and become "like a child."(Lk18:17) Make an active choice of your will to first lead your family in becoming a community. Work on your relationships. Spend time with your spouse and children. Eat meals with them. Talk, think, sing, play, and simply *be* with them. Then take your family and participate in the family of your religious faith and then the greater community at large. Make a difference. In starting this mission, I asked myself what kind of difference my family could realistically make. The reality is that Christ started out with just twelve apostles. There are now over a billion Christians in the world. **With the Holy Spirit, nothing is impossible! Die to yourself! Die to your will! Allow the Holy Spirit to fill what remains and you will change the Earth forever!**

THERE IS A GOD
AND I AM NOT HIM

ONE NIGHT AS I WAS mentally preparing for a Confirmation class I was scheduled to teach several days later, I asked the Lord in prayer if He had any ideas. He responded that evening as I was falling asleep. I was reminded of a scene in a movie called "Rudy" (1993) that I saw ten years earlier. The movie was about a college student who was desperately trying to transfer into Notre Dame University. During his third and final attempt he was praying in the cathedral. An elderly priest sat down to talk to him and Rudy asked the priest if there was anything else he could do to get into Notre Dame. The priest replied, "In all my years as a Catholic priest, I have come to two significant conclusions. First, there is a God. Second, I am not Him."

When I first saw the movie, that line didn't register at all. I do not believe the writer of that movie knew how radically profound that statement is when he was making the film. When thinking about the class I was about to teach, and thinking more deeply about that statement from the movie, I concluded that the statement **"There is a God and I am not Him"** is the most important lesson of my life. "Fear of the Lord" is repeatedly noted to be the foundation of all wisdom in the books of Proverbs, Ecclesiastes, Wisdom, and Sirach in the Old Testament. Fear of the Lord is not running away from God like He is King Kong. Fear of the Lord is simply the understanding of who we are in the universe in relationship to God. Fear of the Lord is the simple understanding that "There is a God and I am not Him!" If you absorb nothing else from this book other than "There is a God and I am not Him," you will be in pretty good spiritual shape.

Looking at that lesson superficially, I thought "Of course I am not God." Then I started evaluating *my* life, *my* priorities, *my* behavior, and *my* beliefs and found that, in many ways, I actually try to *be God* unto myself all the time.

I found I want control of everything. I want to control my time, my environment, my belongings, the people around me, my money, my children, my wife, my job. **In the "Religion of Self," there is no greater thought than that *my* opinion is what matters most.** Especially with regard to sin, I wanted to define the Truth for myself. If I fell short of the "bar of perfection" established by Christ, I would set the bar lower for my convenience. After all, we have all heard from our culture "what is true for you is true for you and what is true for me is true for me." I didn't realize at the time that what that statement really says is that there is *no* Truth, we are all just making it up as we go along. Therefore, with this flawed line of thinking, ultimately the Truth is *relative*. If I am a god unto myself, and you are a god unto yourself, then who is right? Where does the Truth lie? Can the Truth be contradictory? If the principle is that everybody's truth is right, is there such a thing as Truth? In reality, mankind has always searched for Truth. When Pontius Pilate was interrogating Christ, even he asked, "What is Truth?"

I am Roman Catholic. I find many within our Faith saying "I am a Catholic but I don't believe in . . . ." These issues include the Church's teaching on fornication, homosexuality, abortion, divorce, contraception, woman becoming priests, and so forth. Some want a buffet of alternative truths. I want some of this and not some of that. In essence, what I was doing in my youth was making up my own religion, called "Ryanism," whereby I made up truths as I saw fit. What I failed to ask myself was this: if I believe the Church is true in most areas, how did the Church lose its authority in the Truth in areas in which I disagreed?

Many of us live by the standards of behavior we set for ourselves. We make up our own code of morality and we make up our own rules. **If we believe that morality and Truth are relative and individual, we cannot believe in God.** God defines perfection in all areas. He is perfect Love, Mercy, Power, Justice, Knowledge, and Ultimate Reality. **If you** really believe in God, you therefore must believe in *objective* Truth because GOD IS TRUTH!!

In discovering that "There is a God and I am not Him," I began to understand that there is *objective, unadulterated* Truth: Truth that is still true whether I like it or not; Truth that is still true whether or not I have a different opinion; Truth that is still true whether or not I have the ability to live up to that standard. Truth is not a democracy. Truth is not an opinion poll. Truth is *reality.* I have a free will to accept it . . . or reject it and practice Ryanism. If "There is a God and I am not Him," then there is Truth that transcends the desires of my will and what I prefer to make up on my own.

I am not the first person to have a struggle with this basic principle. We have been trying to be God unto ourselves since the beginning of mankind as described in the Bible, Genesis chapter 3: 1-5

> "Now the serpent was the most cunning of all the animals that the Lord God had made. The serpent asked the woman, "Did God really tell you not to eat from any of the trees in the garden?" The woman answered the serpent: "We may eat of the fruit of the trees in the garden; it is only about the fruit of the tree in the middle of the garden that God said, 'You shall not eat it or even touch it, lest you die.' But the serpent said to the woman: "You certainly will not die! No, God knows well that the moment you eat of it your eyes will be opened and you will BE LIKE GODS WHO WILL KNOW WHAT IS GOOD AND WHAT IS BAD."

Sound familiar? Is this not the same situation we face every day of our lives? The first sin was not merely a sin of disobedience. More significantly, it was the *first "original sin"* whereby Mankind first decided to be "like God." I too, have tasted that apple. I grab that apple with two hands and take a big juicy bite out of it every time I desire to be God unto myself. The deadly spiritual principle of *moral relativism,* the failure to accept the objective Truth of God, entered the world that instant.

Trying to *be* God has been the root of all evil on this planet from the very beginning of civilized man. Genesis was written at least two thousand years prior to the birth of Christ and it was traditionally thought to have been referring to a time four thousand years before Christ. As I said earlier, the principles of Scripture transcend time. The principles of Scripture are relevant to mankind today. We are literally asking the same questions and are hungry for the Truth. If the principles of Scripture are true, and God is Truth, then in the depth of our soul we can recognize Truth and still learn from Scripture today.

As a consequence of Man's disobedience to God, and, more importantly, the attempt to be God unto ourselves, death entered the world. As I was growing up, I thought of this as only physical death. I have since learned that it is far deeper than that. When we try to be God, we welcome *spiritual* death into our lives. **Every *sin* is rooted in this desire to be God. Every sin is rooted in pride. Every sin is rooted in self.** Sin is ultimately the spiritual sickness that can cause death to our souls.

Here is the good news. In His mercy, justice, and love, God also gives mankind the path out of physical and spiritual death. In the same chapter in Genesis He says to the serpent, "I will put enmity between you and the woman, and between your offspring and hers; He will strike at your head, while you strike at His heel."

God is already laying out a plan for our salvation in the same chapter of Genesis. He is already telling us about the reality of His only beloved son, His Word, His Truth, entering the world to defeat physical and spiritual death and satisfy divine, eternal justice.

Cardinal Ratzinger, in his last homily prior to becoming Pope Benedict XVI, said "No longer can we live in a world of moral relativism. We have Truth and His name is Jesus Christ!" I heard that line and felt instantly why God would choose him to become our next pope.

Through the fall of our first parents, Adam and Eve, we have all inherited the desire to *be God* in our own lives. I struggle with this on a daily basis. Not only do I attempt to control everything and everyone around me, I even try to control God. If you think this doesn't apply to you, ask yourself this question: The last time I prayed, what did the prayer sound like? I used to pray "God, heal this person. God, help me get a raise at my job. God, let me get an A on my test. God, make this person leave me alone. God, put an end to my suffering." In these scenarios, who is God? If I was trying to be a god even in my prayer life, how many other places in my life was I failing to allow God to be in control?

In my prayer life, like most of the rest of my life, I wanted to control God. If He didn't jump as high as I requested, I would penalize our relationship with doubt. It was like being in a baseball game and I was the coach telling God (the player) what to do. I have since changed how I pray. If one of my children asks me for junk food all day long, I say "no" to prevent them from getting a stomachache. If the same child asks for a piece of fruit, the answer is always "yes." **God will always answer your prayer if it is healthy for you.** I have learned to pray for attributes that will strengthen my soul to allow me to be a better disciple of the Lord and hopefully allow me to enter Heaven for eternity. In receiving these attributes, one can have a glimpse of Heaven *now* with daily, lasting joy. My prayers now consist of asking God to give me strength and courage to do His will. This includes requests for inner peace, patience, fortitude, and humility. In praying for others, I pray that they develop a better relationship with the Lord. I pray to more fully understand the Truth. I pray for wisdom in guiding my family. I have learned to also repent and evaluate my life and my actions. Finally, I simply use prayer to praise God and thank Him for everything. Thanksgiving with praise and adoration is the highest form of prayer. A prayer of thanksgiving is the ultimate prayer of trust and acceptance of the journey I am on with God. It is the ultimate prayer that reflects that "There is a God and I am not Him."

One caution: I have learned to be careful about what I ask for in prayer. I have discovered that most of the virtues and attributes I want come at a cost: *suffering.* Fortitude, patience, humility, wisdom, and so forth are frequently acquired by one making mistakes and then humbly learning from them. Through the humility of suffering, one can be honed like a sword that has been shaped through the fiery pain of the furnace. One becomes spiritually strong.

In preparing for a talk I was going to give to teenagers recently, a thought I received in prayer was that I had to *"die to myself."* If my free will is the only thing that is truly my own, what that really means is that *I must die to my will.* I then thought of a scene from the mini-series "Band of Brothers" (2001). The setting was a battlefield in World War II. One soldier was a hero, running in the open, taking enemy fire at every turn to complete his mission. A second soldier was cowering in a ditch, completely paralyzed in fear. The soldier in the ditch finally asked the hero how he had the courage to run through the battlefield. The hero answered, **"Because I am already dead."**

If we could die to ourselves, if we could die to our will, we would lose all of our fear and become "born again" (Jn 3:3) as fearless disciples of Jesus Christ! If our will could simply and only be to serve the Lord at every moment of every day, why would we have fear? Would we fear how others perceive us? Would we worry about having enough material goods or not achieving worldly success? If we truly believed that God is in control and Heaven is our eternal destiny, would we still fear losing a family member or becoming ill? Would we fear loneliness or worry about how our bodies look? Would we even fear physical death?

The solution to living a life where "There is a God and I am not Him" is to *become like a child* in that relationship. As Christ notes in the New Testament (Mt 18:3); "You must become like a child in order to enter the Kingdom of Heaven." A child has no control. A child looks fully and completely to his or her parents for everything throughout his young life. A child is completely and utterly dependent. That childlike innocence and trust allows that child to be free from worry and fear. No longer is there anxiety about tomorrow. No longer is there an unquenchable drive for wealth and power. A child simply exists . . . wanting to know, love and be with his parents (There's that Baltimore Catechism again!). There is a deep peace and joy in that state of mind. A child truly lives life following the motto "There is a God and I am not Him!"

DUST

"We are dust and unto dust we shall return." This is spoken when Catholics receive ashes on Ash Wednesday. We say this to remind of us the reality that all of the created matter that we experience through our senses of sight, hearing, taste, smell, and touch is simply "passing through" existence. All of this matter has a finite end point. In the end, everything we experience on Earth is dust. "Vanity of vanities! All things are vanity!"(Ec1:2)

Without God, there is no point. Within the Universe, we are simply dust. Our matter does not hold any innate value. **It is only because of God's love *for us* that we become infinitely valuable.** Part of that infinite value comes from being created "in His image." We were not only created with finite matter, but also His infinite Spirit. "The Lord God formed man out of the clay of the ground and blew into his nostrils the breath of life, and so man became a living being."(Gn2:7) As a potter makes a pot from clay, God created us with matter and gave us Himself through His Spirit to make life as we know it. Through His gift of Himself present in our spirit, He therefore created us "in His image." We are literally His children. Although we are born physically from our parents, we are born spiritually from the "breath of God" with an eternal spirit or soul as His gift of Himself to us. It is because our soul's origin as the "breath of God" that *our soul will last for eternity.*

<u>It is the Cross of Jesus Christ that defines our innate value. The Cross is the key.</u> It is through the divine blood sacrificed for me that the Lord reveals how much He values me. I am the lost sheep that the Shepherd dropped everything to find. I am of infinite value not because of anything I have done or will ever do. I am of infinite value because I am a child of God and He loves me enough to lay down His life for

my sin and ultimately my salvation. I am made "in His image" and His breath gives me life. *I am of infinite value because the "breath of God" has infinite value.*

Although I am dust and upon dust I shall return, do not think that I am saying that the matter in which I exist means nothing. Look at your hand. Then, *really* look at your hand. Consider how magnificent the creation of our Potter. We have countless cells working continuously at every given moment. Each cell is like a biological entity in and of itself. It grows, metabolizes, walls off infection, has function provided by the nucleus, and structural support. It ultimately dies and is replaced. Each cell works in union with other cells. Each unique cell has a function vital to the support and well-being of the other cells in the body *without our conscious input.*

Our hand has cells composing marrow then bone. The bones have shapes and joints to enable us to have fingers. These bones are stabilized by ligaments and muscles and tendons. We have 2 sets of vessels, bringing blood to and from the cells in the hand to continue providing the hand with oxygen. We have nerves of sensation and nerves of motor impulses to allow our hand to feel and move. We have temperature gauges within the hand and sensors and signals in the blood vessels which regulate how much blood flow is needed in the hand vs. elsewhere. We have fat and skin with oil and sweat glands that keep the cells of the skin healthy and help regulate temperature. We have hair with follicles and keratin in our nails. Every cell in every part I just mentioned is working at every moment of our existence. Each cell works not only individually, but as a piece to a larger whole.

Why the litany of biology? This is just the hand. Think of how our entire physical body is this complicated in every aspect. Every created biological entity in our world is this complicated. I simply sit in awe of the Creator who can design this masterpiece. Analyzing the complexity of the hand also reveals to me how far many will go to try to avoid belief in God. An atheist would literally have to never look at the fantastic creation of this world, starting with himself, and ignore all that is marvelous about his being. An atheist would have to go *out of his way* to believe there is no God.

I accept that I am dust, and regardless of how marvelous this body of mine is, unto dust this body of mine shall return. With this realization, I can accept how small I actually am in the grand scheme of things, especially in comparison to God. I am just dust. I am just clay. With this thought, **I have also come to the conclusion that there is nothing** *more delusional* **than the thought that my personal opinion actually matters in the Truth and Reality of the universe.**

I am presently writing this book on top of a desk. The desk is a reality. If I do not want it to be a desk, does it no longer remain a desk? If I tell everybody it is not a desk, or we all have a vote that we have an opinion that it is not a desk, in Truth, does the desk cease to be a desk? All of our collective opinions are totally and completely irrelevant to reality.

God is Reality. God is Truth. He does not cease to be in any way because of *our* **opinion of Him!!!** This *delusion of grandeur*, this belief that our opinion actually matters started with the first bite of the apple in the Garden of Eden, "and you will be LIKE GOD and know what is good and bad."(Gn3:5) In short, when we eat the apple, we will forget that there is a God and I am not Him. In short, we will forget that we are just dust. In short, we will forget that the root of all wisdom is "fear of the Lord," (knowing and understanding our place in the universe; that we are dust and He is God.)

It was during this moment of the fall from grace that our physical senses of sight, smell, taste, hearing, and touch became our reality, it became our tool for how we would define for ourselves the Truth. "Then the eyes of both of them were opened, and they realized that they were naked; so they sewed fig leaves together and made loincloths for themselves."(Gn3:7) In the "Religion of Individualism," in the "Religion of Self," we seem to be perpetually trying to satisfy our senses. I have had to ask myself, how many decisions do I make a day that are not to ultimately satisfy one or more of my five senses? How often I make decisions to make me comfortable? How often I am overly concerned with what meal I will eat next, what I will watch on TV, what I will hear on the radio, what I will see on a vacation? We can each fill in our own blank. Although our senses are not innately evil as we were all meant to grow through our senses in a perfect world, working to perpetually satisfy our senses often distracts us from our spiritual, Heaven bound objective. "It is easier for a camel to pass through the eye of a needle than for a rich man to enter the Kingdom of Heaven."(Mt19:24) Why? Because the use of excess money is often only used to satisfy our senses. How concerned am I about what other people think of me, how I look, how much money or power I have? I am so weak. **So much of my life is lived in *total illusion*. So much of my time is wasted collecting, protecting, perfecting, and worrying about dust. So much of my fear and anxiety is ultimately rooted in caring for those five senses.**

In having a decision making process based on my senses, I start thinking "as man thinks, not as God thinks."(Mt16:22) Before the Fall, our decision process was pure. We were not making decisions with our five senses in mind. We were not making decisions to avoid discomfort or suffering at all costs. Instead of trying to be God ourselves and trying to control everything around us to satisfy our senses, we were children of God, completely trusting in Him. If I were to make decisions free of primarily satisfying self and my senses, I would find freedom. I would find relationship with God and others. **Relationships are the only things that are not dust. Relationships are the only things that endure forever. The Trinity is relationship. Love is relationship. GOD IS RELATIONSHIP!**

That is why the bar of perfection in Truth, the Law, is boiled down to 2 statements, "Love your God with your whole heart, mind and strength and love your neighbor as yourself" (because your neighbor is also created in the image and likeness of God as the breath of God is in them.)(Mk12:30) At the moment of our death when we are standing naked in front of God, do you believe any of the dust we cared so much about here on earth will matter? Do you believe piles of money, trophies, awards, degrees, or any part of dust will have any remote use to us at that moment? No. The ultimate question is obvious and simple; did we choose to spend our short time on Earth to develop a relationship with God and the breath of God in others, or not?

How do I build relationships? By serving. Sacrificial love. Death to self! I always seemed to think 2 dimensionally when listening to Jesus in the Gospel. "The first shall be last and the last shall be first in the Kingdom of Heaven."(Mk 9:35) When I was in grade school, I literally thought that this meant I should not fight to be first in line for things. What that really means is **by serving each other, through sacrificial love, we are making decisions free from self, free from the Fall.** In serving each other, we create and enhance relationships with each other and therefore with God.

How many of us have 900 "friends" on facebook? How many of those friends would volunteer to help you this weekend if you had to move? Other than sending an e-mail of condolence, how many would physically show up and visit you if you were in the hospital? Who are the servants among us? Who are our real friends? When I first moved into my first house, a friend of mine volunteered to help me to put up a fence in the backyard in order to keep my children contained in the yard. (Yes, watching my children is like trying to herd cats and fences are most helpful. I am thinking of upgrading to military drones or implanting GPS devices!) That simple selfless act of service brought our friendship to a whole new level. It built a lasting relationship. **Sacrificial love is the antithesis to the "Religion of Self."**

"What you do unto the least of these, you do unto me."(Mt25:40) Living life shedding the shackles of our senses frees us from the "Religion of Self," the "Religion of Individualism." In serving each other, we can truly experience Church, the Body of Christ—God. Only then can we see God with the essence of our being, not just our physical eyes. Only then we can truly serve each other as if they are Jesus to us. Only then, in that relationship with God can we stand before Him naked in our death and have the only thing that endures, our relationship with Him. Only then have we become innocent children once again.

SIN

ONE DAY I WAS SPEAKING to a bunch of priests and I was asked; "Why are so many people choosing not to attend Mass?" My strongly sarcastic answer startled him and most of the room. I replied, "Didn't you know that *everybody* goes to Heaven?" I have been attending very regular Mass for many, many years and have never heard from the pulpit any serious discussions about Hell.

Over the past 50 years, Hell seems to have become a bad word. I am not proposing fire and brimstone craziness. I am simply noting that when the possibility of Hell is never discussed, most people automatically think that everybody goes to Heaven. **If that is the case, if Hell does not exist, then we do NOT have a God that loves us because He is** *forcing* **us to be with Him for eternity. If Hell does not exist, we have no free will and we have no meaning to our lives. If Hell does not exist, then why would we need the grace of the cross through the Eucharist?** Why would we need Mass? Why would we need church? Why seek redemption? Why not be god unto ourselves in the "Religion of Self?"

No, in Truth, *if* we have a God that loves us and is not a slave master, Hell *must* exist. Discussion about Hell is actually a discussion about the *love* of God, because in giving us a free will, He gives us the freedom of *not* loving Him. In giving us a free will, because He loves us, He gives us the freedom of not being with Him. Because His love of us entails our freedom, He endures the pain of separation throughout all of eternity as some of His own children can choose separation from Him. Imagine your own child never choosing to come home to want to know you, love you, or have relationship with you. Imagine giving up your own life on a cross for your child, yet that child uses their freedom to choose eternal death and separation from you anyway. Multiply that pain times infinity and you will understand how much our God longs for us.

If the meaning of life is to choose God, then sin is the alternative choice. Sin is 'missing the mark' regarding the purpose of our life. Sin can be acts, thoughts, or omissions that lead us away from our eternal destination of Heaven.

The root of all sin is pride. It is because of pride that I try to be God unto myself. It is because of pride that I often forget that "There is a God and I am not Him." It is through pride that I want control. Pride always comes before our fall from grace.

To reiterate, if God gave us our lives and our free will to choose whether or not we want to be with Him forever, then there has to be a place we could alternatively choose that would be *absent* of God. That alternative place is called Hell. Imagine a place where there is no Truth, no Standard, no Good, no Beauty, no Order, no Hope, no Charity, no Love, no Mercy, no Justice, and no Light. Imagine every person within this place thinking *they* were God, and, through pride, living the "Religion of Self" to its fullest. Imagine the utter loneliness in a place absent of all community. Imagine the hopelessness in a place you know will never improve for all eternity.

Many ask: If we have such a loving God, how could He ever "send" anyone to Hell? I believe that He doesn't. What is Heaven? Relationship with God. Relationship with the Trinity (which is eternal relationship between the Father, Son, and Holy Spirit). Relationship with the breath of God in others. Family. Community. Church.

When we use our free will to *choose* a life of self, self, self, self, and ultimately self, the natural end to the path of self simply continues on throughout all of eternity. Again, it is actually through His *love* for us that He has given us free will, to choose whether or not we want to be in His presence forever. It is because He loves us that He does not force us to be with Him. If we don't want to be with Him, we therefore choose for ourselves to be our own god and thus we choose Hell; we choose separation from Him. Recall Genesis Chapter 3—The moment you eat of it your eyes will be open and YOU WILL BE LIKE GODS WHO KNOW WHAT IS GOOD AND WHAT IS BAD. **Remember, all** who want to be God get their own kingdom absent of the true God. We call that Hell.

I have had the privilege of hearing about many "near death experiences." A vast majority of the stories I have heard have had experiences that are very, very similar to each other. All of them describe experiences of Heaven or Hell. One thing that repeatedly sticks out about those who describe a near death experience in Hell is the *eternal* nature of it. There is eternal remorse knowing that they wasted this relatively short period of existence called our life. There is eternal remorse in Hell knowing with full consciousness that it will never, ever, ever get better. Eternity is a long time.

My father taught me a lot about the Truth. One analogy he used made a lot of sense to me. Have you ever seen a light bulb on without a shade over it? It is really bright, even hard to look at. It also gives off heat. Imagine God is like that light bulb, always on, giving light and warmth to the world. Imagine sin is like a shade. Every time we sin we choose to place a shade on that light bulb. The light is still on but it is not quite as bright nor is it quite as warm. Then we sin again and choose to place another shade on that light. Pretty soon our spiritual relationship with the Lord becomes darker and colder. It seems to become easier for us to sin and it seems easier to place more shades on that light. Slowly but surely, we soon forget that God, The Light, is on. After putting so many shades on Him, we have now chosen a dark, cold, place for ourselves. We become accustomed to the darkness to the point where, if God is shining through another person, that light hurts our spiritual eyes and we flee from that light. That dark place is Hell.

I have met many people in my life who are already experiencing Hell, this separation from God right here on Earth. They are so enslaved by their sin that they have made a personal Hell for themselves. They become accustomed to the dark. These individuals enjoy the blinding light of the Holy Spirit shining in others about as much as I enjoyed my mother flipping on my bedroom light at 7am on a Saturday morning when I was a teenager. The light hurts their spiritual eyes.

To further understand being trapped in Hell on Earth, talk to any alcoholic or drug abuser. Talk to any person who gave up family and community for wealth, power, and glorification of self. What you will find are individuals who are in the darkness, starving for the next fix of their addiction, feeling enslaved, alone, and utterly empty. Some in the dark are repulsed and lash out against the light and grace offered by others. If you truly allow the Lord to work through you, those in darkness will strive to put you on a cross. Just ask the martyrs. Some, however, are memorized and drawn to that same light, repenting and desiring to start anew. These individuals become God's saints.

The good news about this life is that the light of God is still on. **As long as we still have breath, there is always hope for returning to a relationship with God.** It reminds me of one of Jesus' most well—known parables.

> "A man had two sons, and the younger son said to his father, 'Father, give me the share of your estate that should come to me.' So the father divided the property between them. After a few days, the younger son collected all his belongings and set off to a distant country where he squandered his inheritance on a life of dissipation. When he had freely spent everything, a severe famine struck that country, and he found himself in dire need. So he hired himself out to one of the local citizens who sent him to his farm to tend the swine. He longed to eat his fill of the pods on which the swine fed, but nobody gave him any. Coming to his senses he thought, 'How many of my father's hired workers have more than enough food to eat, but here am I, dying from hunger. I shall get up and go to my father and I shall say to him, "Father, I have sinned against heaven and against you. I no longer deserve to be called your son; treat me as you would treat one of your hired workers."' So he got up and went back to his father. While he was still a long way off, his father caught sight of him, and was filled with compassion. He ran to his son, embraced him and kissed him. His son said to him "Father, I have sinned against heaven and against you; I no longer deserve to be called your son." But his father ordered his servants, "Quickly bring the finest robe and put it on him; put a ring on his finger and sandals on his feet. Take

the fatted calf and slaughter it. Then let us celebrate with a feast, because this son of mine was dead, and has come to life again; he was lost, and has been found." (Lk 15:11)

I see myself in the beginning of this parable living the "Religion of Self." This spiritual "teenager" chooses to leave his home. He decides to leave the authority of his household, to be a god unto himself. He leaves his family community and the relationship he had with his father, essentially saying he wished his father was dead so he could take his stuff.

This teenager then "set off to a distant country," leaving his land and local community. He then "squandered his inheritance on a life of dissipation" essentially choosing to end his relationship with God and leaves his religious community. He wanted control. He wanted to be god to himself. He did not want to answer to anything or anybody.

Once famine struck, he was forced to work at a pig farm in order to survive. This is ironic because, as a kosher Jew, there would be no lower place on earth than working with swine. He was not only working with the pigs, "he longed to eat his fill of the pods on which the swine fed." Symbolically, he was becoming like a pig himself, the most detestable of all creatures during that time.

It is at this moment in the story when the teenager experiences *humility* for the first time. Again, pride is the root of all sin. Humility is the opposite of pride. The moment this youth became more humble through self-evaluation and admission of his error, he began having clarity of thought. His journey of life was instantly turned around and restarted in a positive direction. This turn-around is called conversion of heart through *repentance*.

This teenager had the courage to act on this newfound humility and went back home. His father had never given up on him. **THE LIGHT WAS STILL ON.** Once the son left, the father waited, looking into the distance, hoping for his son to **CHOOSE** to return home. His father saw his son in the distance and ran to him and embraced him, even in his son's 'pigness.' His father was overjoyed at the return of his son and his household (Heaven) was open to him.

God is waiting for you right now. He is ready and eager to embrace each of us in our 'pigness' and welcome us into the kingdom of heaven. All that is needed is *humility* and the desire to 'return home.' We must die to our will. We must become like children, innocent and trusting and longing for home.

CONFESSION

HAVE YOU EVER HAD A bad fight with someone you deeply love? Whenever I happen to be the bonehead who is too stuck on my ideas, desires, and self, throughout the entire argument and afterward I feel awful. I get this queasy feeling in my gut like I would have if I were car sick. If there is no quick resolution, I can harbor a prolonged sense of guilt, anger at myself for fighting in the first place, and resentment to whomever I argued with. **There is nothing emotionally or spiritually healthy about unresolved conflict that damages the only thing that matters; relationship with God or the 'breath of God' in others.**

When I sin, I am in conflict with God and whoever I am hurting. Even if I sin in private, I am still hurting both my relationship with God and others because I belong to the "Body of Christ." I do not exist in a vacuum. If one part of the body is ill, the whole body suffers. It is like trying to walk with a rock in your shoe. Such a small thing can cause such great distraction of purpose for the rest of the body. The whole body suffers when one of its parts is not working to its potential.

Often, I then experience the same moment of pause that the prodigal son had in his 'pigness.' Through evaluation of self in humility, I long to go back to re-establish the relationship I challenged. I long to go home. The Catholic sacrament of Confession is a bastion of grace established at the Cross where we can receive that grace through repentance. Confession is the opportunity for God to embrace us and forgive us as the prodigal son's father embraced him. All Catholic sacraments are physical manifestations of a spiritual reality. Every Catholic sacrament was established by Christ himself. The sacrament of Confession is no different.

Jesus said to them again, "Peace be with you. As the Father has sent me, so I send you." And when he had said this, he breathed on them and said to them, "Receive the Holy Spirit. Whose sins you forgive are forgiven them, and whose sins you retain are retained."(Jn20:21)

Note, Jesus did not say, "Tell everybody to confess their sins directly to God on their own." He sent his apostles out as himself, giving them divine *authority* over sin.

Recall when I described God as like a light bulb that is always on and our sin is like putting a lampshade on that light bulb. Confession is our choosing to allow God to take a bazooka and blow up that shade, allowing his light, warmth, and grace to freely flow back into our lives without hindrance. Imagine having very dirty glasses. As you wear them, you do not realize how dirty they are. When you take them off and hold them to the light, every particle of filth becomes clear. Through the evaluation of conscience prior to our confession, Confession is holding up our 'spiritual glasses' to the light of God.

Confession not only repairs a damaged relationship with God, it heals our relationship with the "Body of Christ." That is why we don't just say sorry to God alone in prayer. The Catholic priest is "in persona Christi" in the confessional: Jesus Christ actually present. The priest then represents both Christ's divinity and humanity in the Confessional—representing both God and "the Body of Christ," his Church.

Several things must be present for absolution to take effect. First, I must be sorry for what I did. Second, it has to actually be a sin (yes, you heard me right. Half the time my wife goes to confess something, the priest sends her home telling her he is not needed). Third, I have to intend on not falling again. Finally, I must avoid the "near occasion" of sin. Before receiving absolution by a priest, a Catholic normally recites a beautiful prayer called the "Act of Contrition."

> "Oh my God I am heartily sorry for having offended thee, and I detest of all my sin because of thy just punishment, but most of all because I offended thee my God, who art all good and deserving of all my love. I firmly resolve, with the help of thy grace, to sin no more and *to avoid the near occasion of sin*."

I have found that I am far more likely to fall into sin in certain situations more than others. Growing up, before my time was absorbed with caring for my family, certain people I associated with would lead me into situations where I would be weak. The reality is that regardless of these bad associations, I am an extremely weak man anyway. Those weaknesses would simply be exploited when I was around those specific people. With this recognition, I try not to "play chicken" with sin. I try not to even place myself in the vicinity where anything bad might happen.

In my profession in medicine, I am surrounded with physically beautiful, lonely, and aggressive woman. My awesome wife, recognizing my challenges declared one day that "I was her lion." I responded, "No dear, I am your gazelle. I see trouble and run my little tail off!"

An alcoholic probably should not hang out in a bar. A smoker probably should not hand out in the smoking section. A gambler probably should not loiter in a casino. I need to avoid situations where I am most apt to be weak in all aspects of my life. Satan knows what buttons to push. His only objective is to draw me away from the mercy of the Cross. His only objective is my eternal soul. Just because I love God, I am in no way immune. Satan seems to spend more of his efforts on me than he used to and he is a worthy and difficult adversary. My only defense is recognizing my weakness, seriously avoiding the occasions where I might be most tempted to sin, and realizing my absolute dependence on the mercy and care of God. I depend on the Cross! I often fall but have no problem crying out for my angels and saints in Heaven to spiritually intercede and help me back on my feet through the grace of the Cross in Confession.

Confession offers very specific grace. It not only offers sacramental grace as the mercy of God. It offers specific grace *to avoid falling to the same sin*. Confession is a very good way to break bad habits. One cannot go too often. John Paul II is rumored to have gone to confession daily.

Again, I am not writing this chapter because I have somehow mastered the secret of avoiding a sinful life. In reality I battle sin and often lose every day. I am usually the guy who gets to talk to my RCIA class about sin because I am the "expert" on the subject through too much experience. When I was in college, I was in the confessional with a super holy priest named Fr. David Testa. He stepped foot onto my college at the Franciscan University of Steubenville as the vocational director and, as a result of his impact, in one year, over 50 young men strongly considered the priesthood. He was the kind of guy that when he entered the room, you would feel the hair on your arm rising. At one point I was in the confessional with him bargaining about my sins. I wanted to know if certain sins of mine were classified as venial sins or mortal sins. As I continued to bargain with him, he finally sat back, smiled, and stated, **"Ryan, for those who LOVE the Lord, there is no difference between venial and mortal sins, because in both cases, you are hurting your relationship with the Lord."**

That was a profound, life-changing statement for me. Why was I always trying to do the minimum? Why did I aspire to be the guy who just sneaks into Heaven at the last minute? Had I not learned that the sin I was still secretly hoping to continue, was hurting my relationship with God? As I noted before, some sins made me momentarily "happy" but would then leave a spiritual hang-over and would certainly never provide lasting joy. I was literally fighting to be able to continue having spiritual cancer in my life. What foolish justifications I have used throughout my life to continue being spiritually ill. It is like a smoker saying he is 'trying' to quit as he still carries a pack of cigarettes in his pocket.

I have learned that prayer and grace from the sacraments, especially the Eucharist and Confession with a priest, is the best medicine. As a spiritual cancer patient, I look forward to the day where I can be free from this disease. In Christ, I feel myself getting stronger. In my journey with Jesus, I am feeling healthier all of the time. Lord, free me of my addiction of self. Free me from the slavery of sin. I depend on you to hold my hand during the difficult parts of my life that I am tempted to wander off your path. Fill me with a thirst to be the man you hoped I could be when you created me. I love you.

GOD WILL TAKE
YOU AS YOU ARE

I AM ONE OF NINE children. One of my six sisters grew up being an all-star. She was good at everything. She got straight A's in school. She excelled socially, athletically, musically, and even spiritually. One day she tinkered with bulimia. This rapidly became a severe addiction. It put severe strains on my family financially, mentally, but especially emotionally. Everybody wanted to help her but we just couldn't find a solution. It was like witnessing a member of your family who you fiercely love drowning in your sight, not reaching up to allow you to pull her out. She was in and out of hospitals without success. She experienced guilt and started hurting herself and began to smoke as well. She began to drink alcohol daily to forget her pain. Ultimately, she entered that dark, lonely, empty place I spoke of earlier: a type of Hell. She would flee from and lash out against those with the light as the light would be blinding in her darkness. She continued on this self-destructive, suicidal-like path for nearly a decade until every moment of her day was consumed by binging, purging, drinking, and smoking. She was at her absolute lowest point. She was in the state of despair. She bought into the lie of *Satan's view of her identity*: a lowly, sinful creature *unworthy* of God's love.

At her lowest moment I sat down to talk with her and she was finally desperate enough to listen. She told me that she believed her sins were so awful that she was convinced she was destined for Hell. I responded that the only person who was keeping her from returning to the house of the Lord was herself. What an arrogant thought to believe that the God of the universe, the God of all creation, the God of life and love wouldn't have the capacity to forgive her sins. I told her to stop fixating on her weakness and her faults and start focusing on the solution which is a relationship with the Lord. **God will take you as you are.** I told her to work on that relationship and put no priority above that. She might still be a bulimic, smoking alcoholic throughout the rest of her life until she dies but God still loves her and wants to be with her above all things. He certainly is not the one that would ever fixate on her faults.

She then focused all of her energy on her relationship with Him and spent over a month in upstate New York in a Franciscan hermitage. This gave her the opportunity to be free from her physical addictions while redeveloping a relationship with God. She went through a "spiritual boot camp," and for the first time in ten years, experienced hope and the love of God. She was once again able to dive into His light and stay there. Through constant prayer and time spent in front of Jesus in Eucharistic Adoration, her demons of bulimia, smoking, and alcoholism have been controlled for many years.

One day I was eating my breakfast as I always do, sharing it bite for bite with my daughter Grace on my knee. I just sat there watching her eat. She was so utterly content. She had complete trust in me. She did not have a care in the entire world. She just wanted to know me, love me, and be with me like that forever. It was so simple. At that moment I felt like how God must feel toward us. I felt totally at peace and, again, experienced true joy.

It dawned on me then why God allowed us to have children. If the meaning of life is to choose God, He could have just made us in our twenties and we could have made the "choice" for eternity and have been finished. Instead, as stated in Genesis: He made us "in His image." He allows us to co-create with Him and allows us to participate in bringing life into this world. I used to frequently ask "what does God want from me?" I think in allowing us to have a family, He has given us a pretty good clue.

God has allowed us to have children so we could have an idea about how He feels about us. Although our relationship with our children is imperfect, and our relationship with our own earthly parents is imperfect, our relationship with God is still very similar. The difference is that His parental relationship with us *is* perfect.

I want my children to be good. I want my children to be upright in character and honor. I want them to be honest, compassionate, caring, helpful, respectful, appreciative, and I want them to always try their best. I want them to live to their potential and to find lasting joy. I want them to uplift everyone around them. I want to be proud of them. I try to focus on their strengths and, if they are truly contrite, I really don't remember their weaknesses. I love them deeply. I believe I would die for them. All I really ever want from them as their father is for them to get to Heaven and *to know me, love me, and freely choose to be with me, even when they are out of the house and they no longer have to.* Is our Father in Heaven so different?

When my son does something at home that I am not thrilled about, I feel sad. The good news is that as long as he is at home, we can work through anything. We have a relationship where I believe he knows I would always forgive him, no matter what. There is no sin he can commit in my household that would cause me to banish him. The greatest tragedy would be if he were to ever *doubt my love* for him and choose to no longer be in my home. As welcome as he would be, he could choose to no longer continue our relationship. I couldn't force him to know me, love me, or want to be with me for eternity. I would still love him. I would long for his return.

Are you home with the Lord? Do you long to know Him, love Him, and be with Him for eternity? You still draw breath. There is still time. God will take you as you are.

THE CROSS

IMAGINE HAVING A GIFT THAT is so special, so spectacular that it took your very life to create it. Imagine this gift was a rope that dangled down into a dark pit where your very own children were temporarily trapped. All they had to do was grab that rope by dying to themselves and thereby opening themselves to this infinite grace transmitted through the rope. That is the cross of Christ.

"He said to them, you belong to what is below. I belong to what is above. You belong to this world, but I do not belong to this world. That is why I told you that you will die in your sins. For if you do not believe that I AM, you will die in your sins."(Jn8:23)

Why was atonement for our sins necessary? It is because we have a God who is Just. Our sin committed has eternally challenged infinite justice. With our first sin, there was injury to an eternal, infinite relationship between man and God. There must be a consequence to our action, not because of what Adam and Eve did in sin, but because of Whom it is they offended by that sin. Their sin created an eternal chasm in the relationship between man and God because God is Infinite. It was through our Fall that we fell into this pit.

Do you believe God is Infinite? Do you believe God is Just? Do you believe God is Mercy? Our forefathers believed in these attributes of God. In the Old Testament, after the fall of man through the first sin of Adam and Eve, man routinely offered sacrifice to God. This was true with Abel, Abraham, and Moses. Why did man sacrifice? It is through the blood of the sacrifice that man would receive finite atonement for their sin. The reason the sacrifice was temporary was that we were sacrificing finite animals to atone for *infinite* Justice.

Throughout the entire Old Testament, the Hebrews repeatedly entered a covenant, an eternal oath, with God. Repeatedly, the Hebrews would break this covenant. It was so bad that God often referred to His chosen people as his "unfaithful spouse." The reason this arrangement was problematic was that His chosen people were human and He is God. They could never live up to His perfect standard. Therefore, the only sacrifice that can truly satisfy infinite or divine justice would be if our atonement was made through divine sacrifice. That divine sacrifice could only be given by God alone. Said best by Dr. Scott Hahn; "God would have to pay a debt He did not owe because man owed a debt he could not pay."

Two of Christ's missions on this planet, as we have discussed, include first coming down from Heaven to show us the "perfect choice." As the Way, the Truth, and the Life, Christ provided a roadmap of perfect behavior in order for us to foster a relationship with God the Father and hopefully join Him throughout eternity. The second and equally important mission of Christ was to be the Divine Sacrifice. In the person of Jesus Christ, and through his crucifixion and resurrection, God has once again revealed His justice, mercy, and love.

Protestants frequently argue that all one has to do is "believe that Jesus died for their sins" and they will be saved. "Whoever believes and is baptized will be saved, whoever does not believe will be condemned."(Mk16:16)

My response is Satan believes that Jesus died for the sins of the world and he is not in Heaven. Do the 'saved' no longer possess a free-will? Are the 'saved' no longer accountable for their actions?

Belief is not simply acknowledging Truth. What does belief mean? "Faith of itself, if it does not have works, is dead."(Jm2:17) Catholics believe it is a combination of faith and works through which one is saved. Belief is not just knowing *about* something. **Belief is incorporation of faith into the *action* of our lives.** That does NOT mean that we can *earn* our way into Heaven through good works. **The Cross is the only font of infinite grace. It is ONLY through the cross of Jesus Christ that humanity can be saved, as his blood is divine!** However, we are *only able to receive* that infinite grace of the Cross through the death of ourselves, which then leads to good works. **The root of all good works**

is sacrificial love. The root of all good works is death to self! Good works, prayer, and the sacraments are the vehicles of grace that open our lives up to the infinite grace of the Cross. It is through good works that we can grab onto that 'divine rope' given to us at the Cross, where our God can then pull us into his presence in Heaven throughout all of eternity.

The Cross not only reveals to mankind the truth of God's justice and love. **The Cross is God's mercy.** There is only one sin in scripture that cannot be forgiven. That is "Blasphemy against the Holy Spirit."

"Therefore, I say to you, every sin and blasphemy will be forgiven people, but blasphemy against the Spirit will not be forgiven."(Mt12:31) Why? Because the Holy Spirit is Mercy! The only way we do not receive the infinite grace of the cross is because we can choose not to accept God's mercy. It is the same sin my sister was flirting with when she thought her sins were "too big for God." God is a gentleman. He will not impose his mercy upon us because mercy is a gift. In dying to ourselves, in dying to our will, we can therefore open our heart and lives to the infinite mercy of the Cross.

One of the greatest ways to open up the infinite font of mercy from the Cross is *to be merciful* to others. In the "Our Father," the prayer Christ himself taught the Church, we pray "Forgive us our trespasses *as* we forgive those who trespass against us . . ." **There is a direct relationship with the amount of mercy we offer to others to the capacity of mercy we then allow ourselves to receive from God.**

Allowing God to shower us with the grace of the cross in our lives through miracles can only happen if we have faith.

> "Jesus said to them, 'A prophet is *not* without honor except in his native place and among his own kin and in his own house.' So he was not able to perform any mighty deeds there, apart from curing few sick people by laying hands on them. He was amazed at their lack of faith."(Mk6:4)

Miracles are a gift from God. He cannot give us this gift of a miracle unless we are willing to receive it. Faith will allow us to receive the miracle of Truth. Truth is God and God is Mercy. Through faith, we can therefore receive the miraculous grace of the Cross, we can therefore receive God's mercy.

The other day I was watching a television program on National Geographic about the universe. The program first noted that satellites we deployed over twenty years ago are just now reaching the fringes of our solar system. To put the size of our solar system to scale, it was noted that if our solar system was the size of an average DVD, then the size of the diameter of the planet Earth relative to the size of the DVD would be proportionate to the size of our galaxy to our solar system. Even more amazing is that the universe has billions of known galaxies. There is thought to be more stars in the universe than grains of sand on the entire Earth. The magnitude of the universe is incomprehensible to our human brain.

Thinking about these facts reminds me about how small I am. I am like an ant—no, even less. I am like the smallest particle of dust.

I spent this past Christmas meditating on the reality that the God of this universe, the God of these billions of galaxies and trillions upon trillions of stars, loved me so much that He became man: God became dust. Not only did the God of the universe become dust, He allowed Himself to be born in a stable: He allowed Himself to be the lowest form of dust. I, like the myriads of angels, shepherds, wise men, Joseph and Mary, can only stand in wonderment at the humility of this God.

Not only did God become dust, but He allowed this dust to torture Him, and ultimately to hang Him on a cross. I simply cannot conceive of the degree of love God has for me. This whole story seems really insane. It goes well beyond my reasoning capacity to try and remotely grasp the insane love that God has for me. I sit and stare at the cross and, in the end, I can only praise Him.

What is even more insane is that this God of the universe would have completed this mission if it were to only save *me*. Christ frequently talks about a shepherd dropping everything to search for one lost sheep. It is much like the God of the universe dropping everything to make sure He found *me* and brought *me* home.

I imagine Satan tormenting in Jesus the Garden of Gethsemane on the eve before His death, whispering in his ear, "Are you sure you want to go through with this? Think of how many people will not accept the grace of your divinely shed blood as a result of their pride and conceit. You will be tortured and crucified in vain.

I imagine Christ at that moment, defiantly resisting temptation as He thought of you and me, hoping in *our choice* for salvation. It is thoughts like this that cause me to find myself madly in love with Jesus Christ, *my* Savior.

Christ did not die to fulfill some abstract distant idea. He died for *ME!* In *my* sin He allowed *me* to beat Him. He stood still as I scourged the flesh from His body. He didn't fight back when I slapped Him. He stood with utter dignity as I spit in His face. He didn't cry out as I pressed a crown of thorns into His scalp. He simply closed His eyes when I drove nails through His hands and feet. He looked into my eyes as I raised Him up to suffocate on that cross.

It is through this same cross that He wipes away the tears from my soul. It is through His shed blood that He forgives me, embraces me, kisses me, and welcomes me home to the eternal feast. I love Him, I love Him, I love Him.

THE CHURCH

AUTHORITY. IN THE REALM OF religion, authority is everything. Every person and every religious institution has an opinion about Truth; the major differentiating factor between them all is authority. It would be helpful to retrace our steps a bit and recall how we arrived at this point. Again, we have logically established that God exists. If He exists, there is obviously reason behind Creation. He has given us clues to this reason: like the capacity to have children so we can understand His motives better. He gave us one thing to call our own—a free will—to choose where we go for eternity. He Himself came to earth as Jesus Christ to reveal to us, through example, the way to make the "perfect" choice. If you have followed this journey of logic, and accept it, then welcome to Christianity!

In this day and age, "being a Christian" is a very broad statement. This generally means that either you belong to the Catholic Church, or to one of 20,000 Protestant churches. In my walk with the Lord, I had to carefully consider which of these paths is most consistent with the Truth espoused by Christ.

I decided that to belong to one of these churches, I needed to have faith in the *authority* of that church to teach the Truth. I asked myself, "If Christ is the Son of God, the Messiah, God Himself, would He have become man, revealed to us the perfect example of Truth, died on a cross, only to ascend to Heaven without leaving any *authority* behind to safeguard that perfect standard of Truth throughout time?" What would have been the point of Christ if, after His ascension into Heaven, that perfect standard of Truth just left the Earth? If Christ did not leave any authority, we can imagine that much of His mission would have been in vain.

It would be like owning a family ice cream shop and making perfect ice cream. The owner of the store knows that one day he will die. Would it not be logical for the owner of the shop to find someone to replace him and pass down the recipe for making perfect ice cream, especially if half of the point of his existence was to bring the world perfect ice cream to begin with? Would he not want the perfect recipe of ice cream to be passed down through ages to come? Would he allow that recipe to die with him, or would he leave *an authority* behind to ensure that the quality of his ice cream would not be diluted over time? The reality is that Jesus did leave an authority. In Mathew 16:15, Christ established the first pope.

> "He (Jesus) said to them, "But who do you say that I am?" Simon Peter said in reply, "You are the Messiah, the Son of the living God." Jesus said to him in reply, "Blessed are you, Simon son of Jonah. For flesh and blood has not revealed this to you, but my heavenly Father. And so I say to you, you are Peter, and upon this rock I will build my church, and the gates of the netherworld shall not prevail against it. I will give you the keys to the Kingdom of Heaven. Whatever you bind on earth shall be bound in heaven; and whatever you loose on earth shall be loosed in heaven."

It was Peter, filled with the Holy Spirit after Pentecost, who delivered a lengthy speech to the gathered crowd, spreading the Truth of Christ throughout the world. The entire early church, including St. Paul and all the Apostles, repeatedly deferred to the authority of Peter. One example of this was at the first council of the church, the Council of Jerusalem:

> But some from the party of the Pharisees who had become believers stood up and said, "It is necessary to circumcise them (the Gentiles) and direct them to observe the Mosaic Law." The apostles and the presbyters met together to see about this matter. After much debate had taken place, *Peter got up and said to them,* "My brothers, you are well aware that from early days God made his choice among you that

through my mouth the Gentiles would hear the word of the gospel and believe. And God, who knows the heart bore witness by granting them the Holy Spirit just as he did us. He made no distinction between us and them, for by faith he purified their hearts. Why, then, are you now putting God to the test by placing on the shoulders of the disciples a yoke that neither our ancestors nor we have been able to bear? On the contrary, we believe that we are saved through the grace of the Lord Jesus, in the same way as they. The whole assembly fell silent, and they listened while Paul and Barnabas described the signs and wonders God had worked among the Gentiles through them." Acts 15: 5-12.

As this passage from the Acts of the Apostles demonstrates, there was much debate, but then *Peter spoke* and the debate about allowing gentiles to directly become Catholic without first becoming Jewish was immediately settled. Within the Catholic Church, since Jesus himself gave Peter the "keys to Heaven and Earth," there has been an authority that has remained throughout history; we call that authority "the pope." The person who presently "sits in Peter's chair" for the church is Pope Benedict XVI. The Catholic bishops are the present day apostles. These bishops have an apostolic lineage of authority that has been passed down through the generations from Peter and the first apostles till now. This lineage is known as Apostolic Succession. **If you believe God is Truth and became incarnate in the person of Jesus Christ, then you should believe in the "fullness of Truth" that has been safeguarded by the Catholic Church for the past 2000 years as Christ himself established the Catholic Church through Peter.**

There have been several councils of the Church over the past 2000 years. All these councils have been similar to that first Council of Jerusalem. There is normally a topic of faith which requires debate and clarification but, in the end, when statements are made by the bishops in union with the pope, a Catholic can have faith in the Truth set forth by these councils. In the teaching of faith and morals, there are always consistent teachings. We can have faith in the Church because of the Church's authority. Without authority, there is only opinion.

The Catholic Church has three "pillars of faith." A pillar of faith is used to reveal the fullness of the Truth on Earth. All three pillars of faith work in unison and are never contradictory. The first pillar of faith is the Magisterium of the Church. This is the teaching authority discussed above which includes the bishops in union with the pope. The members of this group are the shepherds Christ put in charge to guide His Church till the end of time.

The second pillar of faith is the Tradition of the Church. This Tradition is the collection of teachings and customs passed from generation to generation to maintain the words and actions of Jesus—to maintain that "perfect ice cream recipe." This Tradition was maintained through oral history for years and existed *before* the gospels were written and the Bible and New Testament were constructed. This Tradition includes all the divine revelation captured and collected so that every generation of Catholics doesn't have to "reinvent the wheel." There is a significant advantage to having the ability to theologically stand on the shoulders of giants.

Finally, the third pillar of faith is Scripture itself. The Catholic Church believes the Bible is divinely inspired. As Christ recognized the authority of Scripture, so do Catholics.

It is through the combination and union of these "pillars of faith" that the Catholic Church boldly claims to have the "fullness of the Truth." This is not to say that other religions do not contain some Truth. However, some of these religions contain more Truth than others. But the Truth found in these faiths is ultimately the Truth already recognized by the Catholic Church. In the realm of faith and morals, the Catholic Church lacks nothing as the Catholic Church is the Church of Jesus Christ who lacks nothing.

Our Protestant brothers and sisters also have a significant amount of Truth in their faith. Many of my closest friends and relatives come from a Protestant background. (Note that I use the word "Protestant" to refer to all Western non-Catholic Christians.) I have truly learned a lot from these brothers and sisters in Christ. I do not doubt their faith or relationship with the Lord. Too often I am a coward. For the sake of comfort, I miss the opportunity to question my friends on what they actually believe and why. What is funny is that most of these non-Catholic

Christians don't really know what our differences are. Too many times I have missed an opportunity to truly question why we Christians are still divided. Do we not all believe in a Lord of unity? Do we not believe that God desires a unified "Body of Christ?" As I draw closer to the Lord, I often feel that He probably 'rolls His eyes' at our petty squabbles about practically nothing. It is hard to submit to an authority bigger than one's own interpretation of Truth.

At times there are Catholics who attend a local Protestant church service and are impressed with the warm and inviting community atmosphere. There is significant love for Christ in these churches and a significant love for one another. It is this feeling of warmth, coupled with the lack of understanding of their own faith, that cause some Catholics to leave their Catholic Faith for another Christian church. There were times in my walk with the Lord that I thought about converting to a church that was more "active" than my own, or where I liked the music or the preaching better. I would then search for the authority of that church and would discover a great, beautiful, entertaining church built on a *foundation of sand*. I would then inevitably turn my gaze back to Peter "the Rock" and know that I was home.

The word Protestant is actually rooted in the word "protest." The Protestants are in "protest" of the Catholic Church. This protest started in the middle ages when a Catholic priest, Martin Luther, left the church because he was "protesting" the actions of his regional bishop at the time. His concerns with the abuse of political power by his bishop were well founded. Although the Magisterium has the authority of Christ, that certainly doesn't mean that Christ's shepherds are perfect disciples. I often must remind myself that priests and bishops are still human and thus still sinners.

I then remind myself of who Christ picked to be His first Apostles. He picked a variety of men from various walks of life who struggled with sin like everybody else. When you think about it, the first pope of the Church ate and drank with Christ regularly for years. He witnessed first-hand the miracles of the Savior. He boldly allowed himself to be led by the Holy Spirit on numerous occasions. Ultimately, when the moment of truth arrived, Peter denied Christ three times. This betrayal was similar to the betrayal of Judas. The only difference between these two betrayers of Jesus is that Judas believed his sin was "too big for God" and fell into despair. Judas forgot who should be in control; he forgot who was God. In his dark and cold world, where he, Judas, was god, there was no humility, no forgiveness. He therefore hung himself.

Peter took the opposite approach. After betraying Christ, he recognized his weakness *in humility* and repented to God. His soul was saved. It is through weak and humble men like Peter that Christ chose to entrust the survival of His legacy: His Church.

Dr. Scott Hahn often makes a good point: if you have a medical physician that smokes and weighs 350 pounds, doesn't the medicine that the Doctor prescribes still work to heal your physical disease? This concept applies to spiritual health as well. Although our Catholic priests are not always perfect, would it not make sense that the spiritual medicine they provide us through the Sacraments still works to heal our spiritual disease?

Signing up to be a priest during this time is like a man enlisting to the armed forces in a time of war. It takes incredible courage. There is no false pretense about what he is getting into. Although many of our priests are weak men, a vast majority have a singular purpose to their life. That purpose is to bring me and you and everyone they encounter to Heaven by teaching us about Christ and giving us "manna for the journey" through the sacraments. These educated men have sacrificed everything for us. They have given up control of their destiny to their superiors. They have given up a worldly family so they could offer us, the sheep, more of their attention. They have died unto themselves for you and me.

Being a priest in this age is extremely difficult. Imagine serving a parish that used to take 4-6 priests to manage. Imagine living life, practically alone. Since the recent scandal, they cannot even be adopted by a parish family without suspicion. During this time when we are short of priests, entering parish life is like signing up to go onto an island, since it is so much logistically harder to experience fraternity with their peers. It reminds me of a movie called "Cast Away" (2000) with Tom Hanks. In the movie, a very rational, normal guy gets shipwrecked on an island. After a time, he is so lonely that he starts talking to a volleyball that washes up on shore that he names 'Wilson.'

I have at times had rare interactions with certain priests and found that some are a bit socially awkward. Yep, some of these men are talking to 'Wilson.' Then I think about the simple reality that these men have died to themselves. They knowingly chose to go to that island to say 'yes' and have answered the call of the Lord. It is much like the Annunciation when Mary said 'yes' to the Archangel Gabriel. **Through her 'yes,' God became incarnate into flesh as Jesus Christ. Through our priest's same 'yes,' God becomes incarnate into flesh as the Eucharist.** It is through this latter realization that my heart has been opened to total compassion and respect for these men. I love all of these guys, even the ones talking to 'Wilson.' How often I take for granted their presence in my life. How often I have missed the opportunity to thank them for their sacrifice. We all need to invite our priests into our community again. We all need to offer respite from their lonely island.

Tangents, Ryan, tangents! Back to our Protestant brethren. The fundamental problem with Martin Luther rejecting the Church was that, instead of focusing specifically on the abuses he saw with the practical management of the Church, he started to change his core beliefs in the realm of faith and morals to his own liking. His new religion was so uniquely his own, it ultimately came to be called the Luther-an church. He eliminated the first two "pillars of faith" all together and he, like the 20,000 other protestant denominations, believe in only one pillar of faith: that of Scripture alone.

What Luther failed to recognize is that oral tradition came *before* scripture. It was only after the Apostles recognized that the Second Coming of Christ was not likely to occur in their lifetime that the gospels were finally written down. It was the Catholic Church that decided during the Council of Hippo (393AD) and Carthage (397AD) which books of the Bible were "divinely inspired" and therefore included.

By eliminating the belief in any authority and using Scripture alone, Martin Luther set up a system inclined to perpetuate continuous division because *people interpret scripture differently*. Without a Magisterium to provide an interpretation of scripture consistent with tradition, a Protestant church may be in a situation where it thrives only as long as its pastor is present. The moment that pastor leaves, or there is a disagreement or debate about the interpretation of scripture within that church because there is no authority or tradition, there is a risk that the church will break down into more protestant sects. That is one significant reason that there are currently over 20,000 different Protestant churches in the United States. Even within the Lutheran faith, one Lutheran service may be different from another Lutheran service that takes place down the street because again, the entire Protestant faith is based primarily upon the interpretation of scripture by the individual pastor. The Bible was and is a source of Truth. However, without the context of tradition since the time of Christ, and without the shepherds in the Magisterium to guide the flock, the sheep will interpret scripture as they see fit. The Truth is then dependent upon the views of the individual pastor or some kind of democratic process such as a group of "elders."

The reason why many Protestant churches seem to be "on fire with the Spirit" is because most of these churches are first or second generation churches. Most of the people in the church have freely chosen to be there for a specific reason. The question about the teaching message given in a church—beyond all the bells and whistles—is what the church looks like after four or five generations when the members have not freely chosen to join the church on their own accord but were born into the faith. Churches struggle to stand the test of time when the initial zeal has died along with its original members.

Taking a step back and looking into this objectively, do you really think that the Truth of the universe is based on a democratic process? Would Christ have intended on leaving a church with these continuous divisions? Would Christ have left us without a Shepherd? Would He have expected us to individually come to the Truth ourselves without taking into consideration the Truths found by our forefathers? Do we believe we are really the first ones to come up with questions about our faith? Do we believe that no one else throughout Christian history has come up with any answers? **Was Jesus wrong when He stated that "the netherworld will not prevail against it (the Catholic Church under Peter's authority)?"**

At the end of the day, I believe a lot of protestant Christians frequently *act* upon the "Truths" established by the Catholic Church better than some Catholics, whether the Protestant recognizes this reality or not. We are all truly brothers and sisters in Christ. If you are a non-Catholic Christian, I implore you to discover the origins of your protestant sect. I ask that you look for the *authority* of your faith. *When you find that it does not originate historically with Christ Himself*, I implore you to consider returning home to the Catholic family. There are so many people that look at us (Christians) as the enemy. Now, more than ever before, we need to stand as one. Lord, grant us the courage to rationally face our differences with a spirit of love in you. Unify us in this time of division. Help us to die to ourselves so we can open our heart to *your* authority. I trust you Lord.

HOLY COMMUNION

I HAVE LEARNED THAT GOD has given us a time machine that brings us back in time to witness first-hand the Last Supper of Jesus Christ and His crucifixion. We can literally eat and drink with Christ and physically stand at the foot of the cross, gazing upon the Savior who is dying for our sins. We can then come into union with Him, becoming *one* with His resurrected body, blood, soul, and divinity. We can also become *one* with the Church family through the same Communion. We can do this today, right now, at any Mass held throughout the world.

When I was growing up, I always looked at the Mass as a *meal* in which the "Body of Christ," the Church, gathers to build community. I believed that the meal shared at church with the 'Church family' was similar to the meal I shared at home with my family. This is, in fact, true. Mealtime is a critically important opportunity to share with one another, to learn about one another, to encourage each other, to learn about our Faith, to strengthen relationships, and to grow more unified as a family. I can tell you that there is no time more precious at home than the meal time I spend with my family. However, what I discovered in college is that, although we draw closer to each other at Mass in relationship, the essence of Mass is much, much deeper and incredibly profound. I had not yet remotely grasped the magnitude of what actually occurs in this Sacrament of Holy Communion.

The Mass has its roots all the way back to the book of Genesis with Abraham. In short, Abraham desperately wanted a son. He was obedient to God and God established a covenant (a contract) with Abraham. As a result of Abraham's obedience, God promised Abraham "descendants as numerous as the stars."(Gen15:5) Ultimately, Isaac was born. Abraham loved "his only beloved son."

As the story continued, Abraham's faith and obedience was put to the test. The Lord asked Abraham to sacrifice "his only beloved son."

Genesis 22:1-13

Sometime after these events, God put Abraham to the test. He called to him, "Abraham!" "Ready!" he replied. Then God said: "Take your son Isaac, your only one, whom you love, and go to the land of Moriah. There you shall offer him up as a holocaust on a height that I will point out to you . . . Thereupon Abraham *took the wood for the holocaust and laid it on his son Isaac's shoulders,* while he himself carried the fire and the knife. As the two walked on together, Isaac spoke to his father Abraham: "Father!" he said. "Yes, son," he replied. Isaac continued, "Here are the fire and the wood, but where is the lamb for the holocaust?" "Son," Abraham answered, *"God himself will provide the lamb for the holocaust."* Then the two continued forward. When they came to the place of which God told him, Abraham built an altar there and arranged the wood on it. Next he tied up his son Isaac, and put him on top of the wood on the altar. Then he reached out and took the knife to slaughter his son. But the Lord's messenger called to him from heaven, "Abraham, Abraham!" "Yes Lord," he answered. "Do not lay your hand on the boy," said the messenger. "Do not do the least thing to him. I know now how devoted you are to God, since you did not withhold from me your own beloved son." As Abraham looked about, he spied a ram caught by its horns in the thicket. So he went and took the ram and offered it up as a holocaust in place of his son.

This concept of an only beloved son carrying wood on his shoulders to be sacrificed sure sounds a lot like a preview to the crucifixion of Jesus Christ. Considering the reality that Isaac was large enough to carry the wood of the sacrifice on his shoulders and that his father, Abraham, was an old man, Isaac likely offered himself to be bound prior to the sacrifice.

The Jews built Solomon's temple on the traditional site of where that event occurred. When the Jews sacrificed the unblemished lambs in the temple, a ram's horn was blown to remind God that "He will provide the lamb (Jesus Christ)." When John the Baptist first saw Jesus, he boldly proclaimed "Behold the Lamb of God that takes away the sins of the world."(Jn1:29)

The Jewish Passover is another example of the tradition of the "sacrifice of the lamb." In Exodus 12:3-8 we find the verse:

> "Tell the whole community of Israel: On the tenth of this month every one of your families must procure a lamb . . . The lamb must be a year old and without blemish. You may take it from either the sheep or the goats. You shall keep it until the fourteenth day of this month, and then, with the whole assembly of Israel present, it shall be slaughtered during the evening twilight. They shall take some of its blood and apply it to the two doorposts and the lintel of every house in which they partake of the lamb. That same night *they shall eat its roasted flesh with unleavened bread* and bitter herbs."

On Palm Sunday, Christians celebrate Jesus entering Jerusalem. Historically it happened to be the same day that the "unblemished" lambs were likewise being ushered to the temple. At the Passover meal itself the following Thursday evening, Jesus took the unleavened bread "said the blessing, broke it, and giving it to his disciples said, "Take and eat; this is my body." Then he took a cup, gave thanks, and gave it to them, saying, "Drink from it, all of you, for this is my blood of the covenant, which will be shed on behalf of many for the forgiveness of sins." (Mt 26:26-28)

It was at the Passover meal that Christ gave Himself *to be consumed*: body, blood, soul, and divinity just as the Jews would normally consume the slaughtered, unblemished lamb, not only for Passover but also to seal a new covenant.

It was immediately after this Passover meal (the Last Supper) that Christ was taken into custody and condemned. The next day, he was hanging on the cross at the same time that the unblemished lambs of Passover were being slaughtered in the temple. It is believed that Christ died at 3:00 PM.

While I was growing up, I somehow separated in my head the Last Supper event from the Passion: that is, the suffering and death of Christ. In Truth, **the Last Supper is the Passion!** Christ truly is "the Lamb of God." The major difference is that, because Christ is divine, His sacrifice pays the price for our sin and satisfies divine justice.

At every "sacrifice of the Mass," we follow what Christ commanded for us. He stated after the consecration in Luke 22:19, "Do this in memory of me." At Mass we re-present the sacrifice of the divine Son to His Father in Heaven. Even as the priest enters the church, he walks directly to the altar and kisses it, as he is kissing the cross of Christ. We start the Holy Sacrifice by purifying ourselves by repenting of our sins. We say a prayer of contrition called the Confiteor:

> I confess to almighty God, and to you, my brothers and sisters, that I have greatly sinned, in my thoughts and in my words, in what I have done, and in what I have failed to do; through my fault, through my fault, through my most grievous fault. Therefore I ask Blessed Mary, ever virgin, all of the Angels and Saints, and you, my brothers and sisters, to pray for me to the Lord our God.

During the celebration of the Mass, we read four readings from scripture and are then taught by our priest. Then, as the Jews did formerly, we bring our monetary worldly sacrifice to the altar. As one "Body of Christ," we offer the only thing that we have that is our own: we offer to God *our will*. We sacrifice our control. We offer up our daily sufferings, our crosses. We give over to God our desire for all things other than Heaven. We die to our self! We put these sacrifices, these gifts, on the altar along with the Son of Man in order to renew the "New Covenant" that God the Father has with all of us.

The Catholic priest washes his hands as would the Jewish Levite priest before he slaughtered the unblemished lamb. Other than in the confessional, this is the other singular moment when the priest is "in persona Christi," Christ fully present through his priests. On the altar, the Catholic priest offers the Body of Christ and the Blood of Christ *separately* to the Father. (At the last supper Christ did not say this is my body *and* my blood.) When blood is separated from the body, one is dead; we are witnessing the actual death of Christ on the cross at each Mass.

This moment of offering, this moment of consecration, is the moment we are mystically and physically present at the cross: **the same cross as 2000 years ago; the same cross that transcends time with this sacrifice; the same cross that saved me from separation from God and allows me to be able to "come home" to the Lord when the time of my eternal choice comes to an end.** It is through the reception of this "Passover" sacrifice that the blood of Christ, the Lamb of God, is wiped on the doorposts of my soul and the "Angel of Death" can no longer affect my birthright of Heaven.

At Mass, we then proclaim one of three possible responses including, "Save us Savior of the World, for by your cross and resurrection, you have set us free!" At this moment, we are in the presence of the living, *resurrected* Lord in the form of this unleavened bread and wine which has been transformed into the actual Body and Blood of Christ.

We then consume Jesus and, if we are in the state of grace (without mortal sin), we become *one* with Him and *one* in communion with the whole community of believers; we become *one* with the "Body of Christ." I have often told our widows not to concern themselves at length with visiting their deceased spouse in the cemetery as they can still become *one* with them in the "Communion of Saints" at Mass.

In becoming one with Christ, we are given "manna for the journey" of life. The Jews sustained themselves physically on manna (unleavened bread) in the desert. I sustain myself spiritually on manna from Heaven: Our Eucharist. In receiving Him, I have the potential to receive an ocean of spiritual grace that sustains me and helps me to make choices for God. In receiving Christ, the Lord gives to me all the grace I am open to, and capable of, receiving.

Many times at Mass, I cringe as many of my fellow churchgoers do not seem to understand what is going on. Through evident lack of reverence, it is clear that there is some confusion with where they

are, what they are doing, and WHO they are receiving. As they bolt
from the church early to their cars to beat traffic, knocking over old
ladies and cursing, I have often asked myself, "is the Eucharist they just
received minutes ago broken?!!" Didn't they just receive the tidal wave
of grace that God offers in every Eucharist? Didn't many saints literally
survive physically on the Eucharist alone? Didn't others go into states of
ecstasy? **The proportion of grace I receive in the Eucharist is directly
proportional to the amount I have died to myself that can be replaced
by Him.** Some receive an ocean of grace, others just a shot glass.

If you have doubt about the true and complete presence of Christ
in the Eucharist, you are not alone. If you were to ever memorize a
verse from Scripture, the following would be the one to remember. My
Protestant friends who seem to have the entire Bible memorized chapter
and verse generally leave me alone after we discuss John 6:47-69:

"Amen, Amen I say to you, whoever believes has eternal life.
I am the Bread of Life. Your ancestors ate the manna in the
desert and they died; this is the bread that comes down from
Heaven so that one may eat it and not die. I am the Living
Bread that came down from Heaven; whoever eats this bread
will live forever; and the bread that I will give is my flesh for
the life of the world." The Jews quarreled among themselves,
saying, "How can this man give us his flesh to eat?" Jesus said
to them, "Amen, Amen I say to you, unless you eat of the
flesh of the Son of Man and drink his blood, you do not have
life within you. Whoever eats my flesh and drinks my blood
has eternal life, and I will raise him on the last day. For my
flesh is true food, and my blood is true drink. Whoever eats
my flesh and drinks my blood remains in me and I in him.
This is the bread that came down from Heaven. Unlike your
ancestors who ate and still died, whoever eats this bread will
live forever." Then many of his disciples who were listening
said "This saying is hard; who can accept it?" . . . As a result
of this, many of his disciples returned to their way of life and
no longer accompanied Him. Jesus then said to the Twelve,
"Do you also want to leave?" Simon Peter answered Him,

"Master, to whom shall we go? You have the words of eternal life. We have come to believe and are convinced that you are the Holy One of God."

In Scripture, because there was no ability to have bold print or italics, important points were repeated for emphasis. The prior verse was the single most repeated verse by Christ in the entire gospel. Jesus never said the Eucharist was a *symbol* of anything. He was so specific about this Truth that he was willing to allow all of his followers, including his twelve Apostles to leave him over it. His closest friends, his apostles, didn't understand at the time what the Lord was talking about. Peter (as usual) states, "To whom shall we go?" They had faith *without* understanding.

Jesus Christ is fully present, body blood soul and divinity in the Eucharist, whether or not I believe it. Again, there is nothing less relevant to the Truth and Reality of the universe than my personal opinion. Truth and Reality do not bend to my will, as "There is a God, and I am not Him." **Jesus is fully present in the Eucharist because** *He* **said so.** It is really that simple.

Often I have asked myself about this Truth, that is, the true presence of God in this cup of wine or this piece of unleavened bread. In my doubt I ask myself one question, "Where else would I go?" I have accepted the fact that, in this case like many others, I do not know everything or understand everything. I am a spiritual child. I have faith that my Church, my spiritual mother, has my best interests at heart. Like a mother, to the extent I can understand, it is her goal to teach me Truth.

When my children were two years old, I would tell them that the stove was hot. No matter how much the two year old would argue about it, or will it to be otherwise, the stove remained hot. My children didn't have to believe it, or understand it to be true, in order for the hotness of the stove to be reality. Ultimately, if they disobeyed me and touched the stove, they got burned.

My spiritual mother, the Church, is the same. Based on her knowledge of Christ and her 2000 years of collective experience and wisdom, the Church has a thorough grasp of the difference between *healthy* spiritual behavior versus *unhealthy* spiritual behavior. Like my worldly mother, the Church remains with me as a support to comfort me if I touch the hot, spiritual stove and get spiritually burned.

I am not recommending that one remain ignorant about *why* the Church teaches what it does. Through asking questions, I can mature in my faith. I can learn to obey not out of fear that the stove is hot. Instead, I can learn to obey *because I love my mother*. This is how a mature relationship with the Lord and His Church can be achieved. But in the end, because of my trust in the intentions of my mother, the Church, I obey with or without understanding. Later, I may be blessed with the "why" of things when the Lord determines the appropriate time to teach me and I am open to hearing the Truth.

Christ is truly present at every Mass, in every country throughout the world, every day. It doesn't matter if the priest is boring, old, young, mean, fantastic, holy, crazy, or even speaks your language. Nothing else matters other than the fact that *Christ Himself* is there. The Angels of Heaven kiss the fingers of your priest as he holds in his hands the body, blood, soul, and divinity of God. These Angels do not discriminate who the priest is because wherever Christ is present; that is all that matters. The specific celebrant of the Mass is irrelevant to me. I go to Mass as often as I possibly can to receive Christ. The Catholic Church believes we should be nourished by the grace of the Eucharist *at least* weekly and on Holy Days. If Heaven is our objective and grace is what will help to get us there, we should consider making it to Mass daily.

The kids in my Confirmation class often comment that Mass is "boring." I would then explain that God didn't put His cross in our presence to entertain us. I don't attend Mass to be entertained. Rather, I attend Mass to be in the *presence of God* when He suffers and dies for my sins. Once the kids understand that the center of the universe, the ground zero of salvation, is based on this sacrifice of the cross present at every Mass; once they understand they are to offer themselves on that same altar; then Mass is no longer viewed as some form of entertainment, but the truest reality.

It is the grace of the Cross, the grace of every Mass, which unites Heaven to Earth. As much as God is present to us all the time, by coming to us body, blood, soul, and divinity through the Eucharist, God is *uniquely present* to us at Mass. Once I understood the Truth about God's real presence at Mass, my behavior changed. There is no earthly priority that can even come close to the priority of being present a the foot of that Cross. Sleep, sports, family events, shopping, work, and school—*nothing* is more important to my salvation than the reception of Christ at Mass. **If what I am doing is not benefiting my journey to salvation, I am wasting my time.** I would be forgetting the meaning of my life.

When I go to meet God, I try to respect Who it is I am about to receive. I fast from food one hour prior to Mass. I try to arrive early and I don't rush out at the end. I genuflect (kneel) toward the tabernacle before entering the pew and when leaving the church. I dress appropriately for Mass in respect for the Lord who has invited me to His house. I try to focus on what is transpiring at Mass, especially during the consecration. In giving of myself completely in sacrifice, I offer to the Lord my voice at Mass and expect my kids, with voices good and bad, to do the same. I kneel throughout the consecration and bow my head respectfully at the consecration itself. I also bow just before receiving Christ in the Eucharist. In trying to be as reverent as I can be, I also now receive Christ directly on the tongue.

Before receiving Christ in the Eucharist, I need to be ready spiritually. If I have mortal sin on my soul, the act of receiving Christ prior to the repentance of that sin in the sacrament of Confession is a *sacrilege* (a serious sin caused by the irreverent act).

> "Therefore whoever eats the bread and drinks the cup of the Lord unworthily will have to answer for the body and blood of the Lord. A person should examine himself, and so eat the bread and drink the cup. For anyone who eats and drinks without discerning the body, eats and drinks judgment on himself. That is why many among you are ill and infirm, and a considerable number are dying." (1Cor11:27)

If the Eucharist is just a symbol, why would one need to "be worthy" prior to receiving it? If I am not prepared to receive Christ, I must still attend Mass to be with my church family. Again, the only person keeping me out of grace is myself. God wants me home. He even wants me home if I am covered in sin. As I mentioned before, all venial (non-serious) sin is forgiven upon the reception of the Eucharist.

The Lord loves to be present fully to His children at the Mass. One evening my youngest sister (as an adult) decided she was going to sleep late and miss Mass the following morning. I told her, "The Lord expects you to be at Mass." She laughed and said, "Prove it." I said, "God will wake you up and not allow you to fall back asleep." She is a very deep sleeper and didn't take my comment seriously. The next morning, true to my prophecy, a large fly buzzed around her room and landed repeatedly on her sleeping face. It finally bothered her enough that she got up in time for Mass and decided to attend. She later thanked me for 'kicking her in the butt' and has attended Mass at least weekly since then.

The time machine God has given to all of us is such a blessing. To be back in time with Christ at the time of his death we have the opportunity to truly know Him "through the breaking of the bread." (Lk 24:35)

PRAYER

Relationships are the only things that transcend time and last forever. Relationships are the only things that are not dust. In all relationships, communication is paramount. This is especially true with spouses and children. It most definitely applies to our relationship with God.

Without communication, relationships die. Just ask any divorcee or child who is distant from a parent. I have found that my relationship with God is no different. *Without* prayer, it would be like telling the Lord, "I love you. I will give up everything for you. I just don't want to talk to you, think about you, listen to you, or be around you."

Prayer is simply communication with the Lord. This communication doesn't mean I always need to use words. Sometimes I just sit with my wife. We don't need to talk about anything. We just hold hands and sit together. We are *present* to one another. This communicates to her that she is important to me. This lets her know that there is nothing more important to me at that moment than her. This gives me a moment where I might be more apt to listen.

Similarly, I sometimes just sit with the Lord in what is called Adoration (or Exposition) of the Eucharist. It is like sitting on the porch with my wife. To enable Adoration, a consecrated Communion Host—that is the body, blood, soul, and divinity of Jesus Christ—is placed by the Catholic priest or Deacon in a transparent receptacle called a monstrance. I just sit there in His presence. Sometimes I talk; sometimes I listen. In all cases, being with Him in person is like getting a suntan of grace. There is something special about stopping my life for a moment to simply *be* with the Lord. Like taking a pilgrimage, God seems to appreciate the effort. He rewards my life with peace and joy, no matter how tough things of the world are. Now that doesn't mean I don't have normal anxiety about my worldly responsibilities. In prayer, God simply re-centers my priorities and gives me the grace to endure.

In many ways, my whole life is a prayer. Each morning I offer up my day to the Lord to do with me as He wills. I ask Him to help me to have the courage to die to my will. I offer up the challenges He places before me and I ask for the wisdom to never miss an opportunity to bring others to Him. I live my life with an acute awareness that *there are no accidents*. I ask to become aware of the purpose of the present moment and try to learn from every situation the Lord brings me.

In my journey of life, I often reflect on my day and ask God to identify those areas in me that need the most correction. Prayer is like an x-ray for the soul. I have so many weaknesses. However, with the insight God gives me, I am able to focus my prayer and ask for the grace (spiritual medicine) to address my specific spiritual illness in sin.

Other than the Mass itself, the greatest prayer I have ever encountered is the prayer of the rosary. The rosary is an organized prayer by which I am able to think about various times of Christ's life. The genius of the rosary is that by reciting the "Hail Mary's" and "Our Father's," it creates a disciplined amount of time where I am meditating on Christ's life. Through that meditation, I can learn to emulate that perfect example. Beyond that, is too complicated to describe how to pray the rosary in this book. My advice would be to research how to pray it or ask your priest. It will change your life.

Praying the rosary is a powerful spiritual weapon. Satan hates it. I start praying the rosary at times when I am tempted; there seems to be nothing more effective in refocusing my mind on my master and friend, Jesus Christ. It is a prayer that opens a font of grace in my life.

Let me tell you a secret. I really don't enjoy praying the rosary. It takes a lot of discipline. The rosary is a spiritual *exercise*.

I also don't like physical exercise. There is nothing I like to do less than run on a treadmill. However, I do it because it makes me physically healthy. After I work out, I feel great. I feel physically fast and alert and ready for the physical challenges of that day. If I miss my regular workout, I feel physically slow and dull and out of shape when I am physically challenged that day.

Praying the rosary is similar to that physical exercise. When I pray the rosary, I feel great. I feel spiritually fast and alert and ready for the spiritual challenges I will encounter that day. If I miss the rosary, I feel spiritually slow and dull and spiritually out of shape, not ready to face the various spiritual challenges I am bound to encounter that day.

I used to have long periods of my life where I would literally forget to pray. I would be so wrapped up in my daily routine of life. I would frequently intend to set apart time to pray but as I am easily distracted, I would simply forget. If you have an intention to draw closer to God, He has given us daily tasks that we *must do* so we might as well pray then. We all eat a number of times each day, we drive everywhere, and we spend time in the bathroom (yes, God is even there). Those are the automatic times we are guaranteed to have every day that we can develop the habit of praying. For me, driving is the time when the rosary is the most palatable for me and I am able to successfully have the discipline to do it.

I find I am best able to listen to God when my senses are the most irrelevant. I found my senses serve as a huge distraction. When I am trying to fall asleep, my eyes are closed, the room is quiet, I am not moving, eating, or smelling anything. That moment is the time I can best pray and listen to my thoughts. For the same reason, the next best time for me to listen is the moment when I first wake up in the morning.

"A strong wind was rending the mountains and crushing rocks before the Lord—but the Lord was not in the wind. After the wind there was an earthquake—but the Lord was not in the earthquake. After the earthquake there was fire—but the Lord was not in the fire. After the fire there was a tiny whispering sound. When he heard this, Elijah hid his face in his cloak."(1Ki 19:10)

Why would a man wake up before dawn and sit freezing in a tree for hours when hunting? Because he is able to best hear God's "tiny whispering sound." Menial tasks like fishing, gardening, cutting the lawn, and knitting creates a mindless busywork which allows our minds to wander and talk to the Lord. Don't tell my wife (whisper: or else I won't get any credit), but in order to allow my mind to clear, at times I prefer to disappear on my tractor to mow the lawn. Yes, I am weird like that.

I used to be resistant to organized rote prayers, such as the "Hail Mary" and the "Our Father." I thought to myself, "if I were trying to cultivate a relationship with my wife and kids, and they started to talk to me in some type of prepared speech all of the time, my relationship probably wouldn't be strengthened much by that."

That way of thinking is somewhat valid. If my prayer life was simply a robotic routine of organized prayer alone; if I never made any personal connection to Jesus or accepted His sacrifice for me personally, then my relationship with Him wouldn't be a relationship at all. It would *only* be a religious routine. If I never talked to the Lord using normal conversation, I would have an impersonal relationship with my God.

On the other hand, when I have the discipline to set aside the time to pray with organized prayer—when I have *spiritual discipline*—I find that I will simply talk to the Lord more often than I might otherwise. Without that spiritual discipline, I often become spiritually apathetic. Again, I get so caught up with the routine of life that I simply forget to talk to the Lord. There are also times when I simply don't have much to say. These are the times that we can say the prayer Jesus Christ himself taught us, the "Our Father" or ask Mary, our spiritual mother, to pray with us. These prayers are crucial for our spiritual journey and provide us grace: the spiritual nudge to make the right choices for God.

In the end, making time each day to start with the spiritual exercise of organized prayer can lead to more time when a spontaneous conversation can occur. It is like going on a date with my wife. We can talk at home anytime we want, but in the chaos of the home life, we can go days without a focused conversation. Fortunately we then have the relationship discipline to regularly stop our routine, go out on a date, and just *be with* each other. We may or may not have a productive conversation every time, but, by going on a date, we are giving ourselves a specific time when a great conversation can occur. In all cases, a date is healthy for our elationship.

A disciplined prayer life is like going on a date with the Lord. It is time in the day that I set aside and I pray my organized prayer. Sometimes this leads to spontaneous prayer; sometimes it does not. In all cases, organized prayer is healthy for our relationship. A disciplined prayer life is needed to stay on track.

There is no greater place to experience the combination of both organized and spontaneous prayer than the Mass itself. At any Catholic Church I might attend throughout the world, at any given moment, the essential prayers are consistent at the Mass and the format is essentially the same everywhere. It is truly the "Mystical Body of Christ" speaking and praying in one voice to the Father, "Remember the sacrifice of your only son. Remember your covenant to us through His divine blood."

There are times during the Mass when we pray spontaneously. This is most evident around the time of receiving Jesus in the Eucharist. This is the moment of my life when I am truly closest to God and I pour my soul out to Him. Mass is the cornerstone of my prayer life. It is central to my life, the life of my family, and the life of my spiritual wellbeing. There is no prayer that is more important or that provides more grace. In Mass, my prayer transcends words and thoughts. In receiving the Eucharist (Christ's body, blood, soul, and divinity), my entire being, including my physical being, is in prayer to the Lord. He is *in* me, and I am *in* Him. It is similar to the deep communication, the deep communion, which occurs between a man and wife during the marital act. It is a complete and total giving of all aspects of self: mental, emotional, spiritual, and physical. There is no deeper communication than that.

Through prayer, the Lord has changed my life. He gives me ideas, answers questions, gives me tasks to accomplish, and reminds me of His love for me. I pray right now that the Lord remain with me during this current task. I pray that I write what He desires me to write. I ask for His blessing to rain down on all the readers of this book. I pray that we can all experience His peace and presence now and through all eternity. Amen.

MARY

I TRULY LOOK FORWARD TO teaching RCIA (the Rite of Christian Initiation of Adults) when I get to introduce the class attendees to their spiritual mother. I have the same type of excitement now when I get to introduce you to her as well. To me, it is like finding a child who lost their mother in some tragedy, and then helping to reunite them.

I was introduced to my spiritual mother in the eighth grade. At that time one of my older sisters was the family rebel. She was a typical teenager, depressed and angry at the world. Most of that anger was directed at my parents. She seemed compelled to break every rule my parents made. She was clearly searching for something to fill the void of emptiness when the "success of the world" did not offer the lasting joy she had been promised by the world.

She ultimately read a book about Medjugorje, Yugoslavia, where the Blessed Mother is been believed by many to be appearing to six young children. She felt compelled to travel to Europe, across the entire world in her search for **Truth**. She found what she was looking for . . . She found Jesus Christ there in Medjugorje! She had a miraculous experience. When she returned, she was unrecognizable as my sister. Suddenly she had peace in her soul and a purpose to her life. She started to serve others and was no longer depressed and angry. Her change was so radical that my father took note and was dumbfounded. He started to read a lot about our Catholic Faith. Then, as the shepherd of our family, he began his new journey and, together with my mom, brought the rest of us closer to Christ in a personal way. I can assure you that without the experience my sister had in Medjugorje, I would not be writing this book today.

Who is Mary? Mary is a hero! She is a hero's hero. She is "the New Eve," one of God's greatest gifts to His children. She is the greatest spiritual warrior, the exemplification of humility, the intercessor, the Immaculate Conception, the Queen of Heaven and Earth . . . She is the Mother of GOD.

God refers to Mary, the "New Eve", directly after the fall of man. When denouncing Satan, the serpent, God states in Genesis 3:15—"I will put enmity between you and the **woman**, and between your offspring and hers: He will strike at your head, while you strike at His heel."

God again speaks of Mary over seven hundred years *before* she was born in Isaiah 7:13-14:

"Then he said: Listen O house of David! Is it not enough for you to weary men, must you also weary my God? Therefore the Lord Himself will give you this sign: the **virgin** shall be with child, and bear a son, and shall name him Immanuel."

God then describes this man in Isaiah 53:2-7:

"There was in him no stately bearing to make us look at him, nor appearance that would attract us to him . . . Yet it was our infirmities that he bore, our sufferings that he endured, While we thought of him as stricken, as one smitten by God and afflicted. But he was *pierced* for our offenses, crushed for our sins, upon him was the chastisement that makes us whole; by his stripes we were healed. We had all gone astray like sheep, each following his own way; But the Lord laid upon him the guilt of us all. Though he was harshly treated, he submitted and opened not his mouth; *like a lamb led to the slaughter* or a sheep before the shearers, he was silent and opened not his mouth . . ."

God calls on Mary for the first time at the Annunciation: Luke 1:26-38:

"The Angel Gabriel was sent from God to a town of Galilee called Nazareth, to a virgin betrothed to a man named Joseph, of the house of David, and the virgin's name was Mary. And coming to her, he said, "Hail, favored one! The Lord is with you" . . . "Do not be afraid, Mary, for you have found favor with God. Behold, you will conceive in your womb and bear a son, and you shall name him Jesus. He will be great and will be called Son of the Most High, and the Lord God will give him the throne of David his father, and he will rule over the house of Jacob forever, and of his kingdom there will be no end." But Mary said to the Angel, "How can this be, since I have no relations with a man?" And the angel said to her in reply, "The Holy Spirit will come upon you, and the power of the Most High will overshadow you . . . Mary said, **"Behold, I am the handmaid of the Lord. May it be done to me according to your word."**

With that final statement, Mary did what Eve would not. She *gave up herself* to God. She gave up control of her life. She gave up control of her future with her betrothed husband. She gave up her will and desire. She gave up her name which would be tarnished due to assumed sinful humiliation. She knowingly gave up her life, recognizing that the law of the Moses would have her stoned to death for being pregnant out of wedlock.

She did this all, defeating Satan at that moment who would have tempted her like Eve to "be like God" unto herself—to take control of her own life and destiny. Instead, through utter and complete humility, *Mary died to herself*; Mary allowed herself to be totally dependent on God. She allowed herself to be a child of God. She gave up control of everything, including her fear.

As all of mankind entered suffering and death through the actions of Eve, all of mankind is redeemed and can now enter eternal life through the actions of Mary. This is why she is referred to as the "New Eve."

She is also Satan's biggest nemesis. Satan was once the highest Archangel named Lucifer. He was the highest form of God's creation. It was because of the plan revealed to the Angels of the incarnation of

God, God becoming man (dust), that Lucifer, along with one third of the angels, chose to no longer be with God. He could not humble himself to serve man. Through his spite, his objective was, is, and forever will be, the pursuit of separating God's children from Him.

Satan is the tempter and the liar. Through the experience of my own weakness I can assure you that he is very good at his trade. That is, of course, until he met the likes of Mary. He had never been beaten by a human being. He can lose to Jesus, the Son of Man. However, he has a really hard time losing to Mary. It is through her humility that she personifies everything he is not. It is through her humility that God has elevated her to Queen of Heaven and Mother of God. As she stands firm in her humility, Satan can only "crawl on his belly" in "Eternal Fire" in rage and envy. After all, she only had to say 'no' to God and the Redeemer may never have been born.

As fantastically amazing as Mary is, **she has no power of her own.** Like the moon, she can only shed light on the world by reflecting the Son. She is always taking her children to Him. She is always there, lighting our path to Him.

What is clear is that Jesus listens to her. He followed the Ten Commandments and "honored his father and mother."(Ex20:12) One example of this was during the wedding feast at Cana. According to John 2:3-6, "When the wine ran short, the mother of Jesus said to him, 'they have no wine.' Jesus said to her, 'Woman, how does your concern affect me? My hour has not yet come.' His mother said to the servers, 'Do whatever He tells you.'"

This story tells us a lot about the relationship between Christ and the "Woman." First, like God the Father in Genesis ("I will put enmity between you and the Woman"), Christ always refers to his mother throughout scripture as "Woman." Second, Christ obeyed his mother even though his hour "has not yet come," allowing her to intercede for the bride and groom. Finally, she instructed the servants to "do whatever He tells you."

This entire story is a microcosm of Mary's role in the universe. Mary intercedes for us. While raising nine kids, my mother's instinctual answer to the constant barrage of requests to her throughout a day was 'no.' That instinct of hers usually kept most of us out of trouble. We all knew that if we really wanted something, we could always pass the request through my father. He would intercede for us and, at times, the outcome would be quite different.

Mary intercedes for her children like this all of the time. There is no better person one could have whispering into the ear of the Lord than His mother. When Catholics recite the 'Hail Mary,' we are simply asking the Mother of God to intercede for us at the two most important times in our existence, "now and at the hour of our death." It is similar to asking your wife, cousin, mother, or friend to pray for you, like we all do when we are sick or facing challenges. The prayer to ask for the intercession of Mary has a bit more influence with our Lord however.

It would be foolish to "worship" Mary. Why would someone worship a creature other than God, especially if that creature had no power? Catholics do not worship Mary. Catholics *honor* her. If we want to be like Christ in all ways, we must honor His mother. This is especially true because He gave us His mother, His final gift from the cross, before His death.

During crucifixion, one would normally die through suffocation rather than by bleeding to death. This occurred because as one would hang on the cross, their arms would be stretched straight over their head and, over time, they would not be able to support their own body weight. In order for Christ to fully breathe, much less speak, He would have to pull on the nails holding His hands and push on the nail through His feet to elevate Himself on the cross in order to inhale enough in order to speak. In other words, it took a lot of effort and pain for Jesus to speak while He was hanging from the cross. It is because of this reality that I pay close attention to the few words of Christ while He was on the cross.

> "When Jesus saw his mother and the disciple there whom he loved (John), he said to his mother, 'Woman, behold, your son.' Then he said to the disciple, 'Behold, your mother.'"
> John 19:26-27.

Jesus Himself gave us His mom to be our own. We all have this great mom who wants nothing more than for us to know her Son. She wants nothing more than for us to spend eternity with God and our eternal family in Heaven. I talk to Mary every day. I am a "mama's boy."

Jesus is not jealous of my love for her. It would certainly strain any relationship I would have with one of my friends if I brought him home to my house and he didn't honor, respect, or even want to talk to my mother. Jesus is the same. If I really want to love Christ; if I really want to know everything about Him; if I want to become one with Him; I need to know His mother.

Throughout time, Mary has appeared to visionaries in several places on Earth. In each one of these miraculous appearances, her message always points to her son saying "Do whatever He tells you." Before you shake your head and question the authenticity of these visions, you should know that the Catholic Church is the most skeptical party before declaring one of these visionary sites to be authentic. The Church launches full investigations which often take decades before declaring a miracle.

Many Catholic pilgrims flock to these sites where visions have occurred. These include Fatima Portugal, Lourdes France, Guadalupe Mexico, and Knock Ireland. The Church has yet to recognize Medjugorje because the visions are still believed by many to be occurring today and the investigation by the Church does not begin until the purported visions have ceased.

Following in the steps of my sister, many others in my family have since visited Medjugorje. Some have returned with more dramatic life changing stories than others. All have returned with a closer relationship to Christ from the experience. In going to Medjugorje, or making any pilgrimage for that matter, God seems to recognize our effort to know Him better. It is like in Scripture how the woman pushes her way through the crowd just to touch the hem of Jesus' cloak and was healed from her hemorrhaging. God seems to honor those who are willing to stop for a moment of their life and make a journey to see Him. He seems to bless those who have the faith that "if they were to only reach out and touch His cloak, they would be healed."(Mk 6:56)

When I think of Mary at the foot of the cross, I often try to put myself in her shoes. Can you imagine watching *your* child being beaten and tortured in front of you? Can you imagine the love of your life having a crown of thorns banged into his scalp, having nails driven through his hands and feet, and hung up like a criminal? Could you imagine a mother's instinct to simply want to hold her son who is suffering, wipe the blood from his face, and kiss him like she would have when he was a boy to make him feel better? As was foreseen by Simeon at Jesus' circumcision, her heart was truly pierced as she was tortured, sharing her son's pain. (Lk 2:34)

Better than anyone, Mary understands God's sacrifice for us. She is truly an example to all of us. In the end, I speak to Mary as first did the Angel Gabriel and Elizabeth (Mary's Aunt):

> "Hail Mary, full of grace, the Lord is with thee. Blessed art thou among women and blessed is the fruit of thy womb, Jesus. Holy Mary, Mother of God, pray for us sinners now, and at the hour of our death. Amen."

SAINTS

I WORK A LOT WITH youth. I often hear from co-workers, "Look out for that troubled kid; he or she is a real handful." I take their advice and look out for them, but not because I think they could harm me. I look out for them as potential fantastic saints for God. These upstarts frequently have spirits that are bold and rebellious. These kids have a lot of energy and they are not afraid to use it.

I concluded that there is a lot of courage in rebellion. I know that the trick with these kids is to simply change what they are rebelling against. I convince them that their energy is great if used for the right purpose. If they could rebel against sin; if they can rebel against unhealthy cultural norms, they might end up being the greatest saints ever.

A saint is defined as anybody who is in Heaven. This includes all people who are with the Lord and it also includes the Angels. All the Saints and Angels are members of the "Body of Christ." Some of these members, by the authority bestowed upon the Catholic Church, have been declared Saints (what the church looses on earth is loosed in heaven, what is bound on earth is bound in heaven. Mt 16:5). Ironically, the Church with all of its authority has never declared an individual damned to Hell.

I would consider every *practicing* Catholic in today's society a rebel by default as our American cultural "norm" has deviated so far from Christian principles. Those who are Christian are now persecuted, ridiculed, and regarded as 'unenlightened.' Our media, Hollywood, public schools, colleges, and social elite have essentially labeled Christians as the 'enemy.' This is not the first time we have been persecuted, nor will it be the last.

Jesus Christ Himself was a massive rebel. He was an upstart to man's perception of Truth and societal rule. He was such a rebel that the people "hung Him on a tree."(Acts5:30) I often note that I am probably not standing up for the Truth as boldly as I should, because I have yet to be martyred. With the way things are going, who knows? That day may not be as far off as I once imagined.

God never gives up hope for us. God has transformed some of the worst sinners into the greatest saints. For example, St. Paul literally hunted down Catholics and had them killed. He was on the path of self until the Lord knocked him off his horse. "Saul, Saul, why are you persecuting me?"(Acts 9:4) Paul then redirected the energy he invested in finding and eliminating Christians to telling the world about Christ and the Truth.

St. Augustine, a Doctor of the Catholic Church, makes even teenagers of our generation look like a bunch of Mother Theresa's by comparison. He simply directed the energy he spent on constant partying and sinful living to the new objective of knowing and loving the Lord. This was likely the result of his mother, Saint Monica, interceding for her son in prayer. She prayed for twenty years for his conversion of heart. Finally her prayers were answered. St. Augustine decided to come out of the darkness into the light. He eventually became a Bishop.

Some saints, however, have been saintly from the outset. St. Theresa, often called "The Little Flower", didn't ever seem to have had a dark, sinful time throughout her life. She died at a young age, but her simple writings were so profound that she is also honored with the title "Doctor of the Catholic Church."

The point is that **every human being, regardless of what they have done before, is called to be a saint now!** This is not some calling or expectation for everyone but me. This is not the call only for "holy people." This is God's expectation for me and for every person on Earth.

That Truth was hard for me to accept for a long time, but, in the end, I know that if I want to be in Heaven with God, this is my vocation: to be a saint. I have no higher calling in my life. As a husband and father, I have a responsibility to help my wife and children respond to their calling to that vocation as well. I remind my wife to pray. I teach my children to pray. Attending Mass is mandatory until they are old enough to move out. I educate my children about the Faith. God is the center of our family life. My wife has the burden of calling me to be better than I always want to be or think I could be . . . . Why do we do all this? Because I love them and they love me. I want them to get to Heaven. I hope to be with them all for eternity in the arms of our Lord. If they are not there, even though they still have a free-will and must ultimately make the choice for God on their own, I will have failed in many ways. It is *my responsibility* to ensure that the eternal choice they are making is clear. It is my responsibility to expose them to the Truth. It is my responsibility to introduce them to Christ, whether or not they are interested in hearing about Him, at least until they are 'out of my house.' If I have not made the path to Heaven obvious, I have failed in my most fundamental vocation as both husband and father.

I have encountered many saints in my life. They will likely never be officially recognized as saints by the Church, but they inspire me to holiness by their example and words. These people push me further than I would be inclined to push myself. They care about their eternal destiny. They love others unconditionally. They take the advice of St. Francis and ". . . preach all day and, if absolutely necessary, use words." Their lives are sermons. They rise above adversity and remain steadfast in their journey to eternal life with God.

As part of the "Body of Christ," the saints pray for us and with us. Like other members of our earthly family, we can ask them to pray for a special intention or ask for their help and intercession for us. Similar to our prayers to Mary, we do not pray to the saints like we pray to God. We do not worship the saints; they are not God. We talk to them as I am talking to you right now. They have no innate power. They simply can join with us and pray *with* us to God.

When there is an illness in the family or when I am going to take a big test, I ask my family to pray for me. The saints and angels in heaven are part of my family too. As a part of my family, they care about me and the decisions I make in my life. They are my biggest cheerleaders, rooting me on to make healthy choices.

Angels can physically and spiritually intervene in our lives. They are our protectors. We each have at least one guardian angel (Catechism of the Catholic Church: 336). We have all had moments in our lives when we have experienced unexplainable circumstances and have been spared suffering and death. For some reason in those situations the Lord utilized our angelic help to keep us around a bit longer. Obviously it was not yet our time. I pray that we learn to recognize God's intervention in our lives through our angels. How often I see people miraculously survive an illness or accident and shrug their shoulders, thanking "luck" for their life. During these occasions in my life when I have been spared, I pray that I have the grace to use the remaining time on this earth the Lord has given me to serve Him well.

It is an amazing thought that when I am in Mass, the church is full of legions of angels, praising and glorifying God with me. Members of our family that have made it to heaven pray with us throughout the sacrifice of the Mass and become one with us during our reception of Holy Communion.

Saints are not people who never sin. Saints are people who have fallen to sin but keep getting up! They never give up. They do not allow themselves to forfeit to despair. They do not "blaspheme the Holy Spirit" by denying in their lives the Mercy of God through the Cross! They do not allow themselves to become apathetic to sin. They have hope in God's mercy and thus hope in their salvation. **Ultimately, every saint has a past and every sinner has a future. YOU were created for sainthood!** It is that simple. Have you answered the call of that universal vocation? I often challenge myself, questioning if I am living a life worthy of that title.

I pray that I might learn from those who have gone before me. I pray that, through God's grace, I can one day join my brothers and sisters in the arms of our Lord. I look forward to meeting all the people that influenced my opportunity to see God. I am excited to meet my angels. I thank God for the saints!

SUFFERING

Reality: we are all going to suffer at some point in our lives. The suffering may be physical, emotional, spiritual, or mental. As much as we try to avoid it, cover it up, or fear it, we will all suffer at some point. What a bummer.

I am not exactly an expert at suffering. The Lord has so far allowed me to live a pretty cushy life. I am not writing this chapter claiming I have somehow found a way to be impervious to suffering. I dread suffering as much as the next guy. Ask anybody who has seen me with the stomach flu; I am a pretty big wimp. That being said, in my short life the Lord has taught me a lot about suffering.

First, it is through the consequences of the original sin of Adam and Eve that man brought death and all its related aspects into our world. God *allows* this consequence of sin to exist. As such, a significant amount of the suffering mankind endures is self-inflicted, either through the consequence of one's personal sins or through the sins of others. It is through God's love of us that he gives us a free-will.

As I mentioned earlier, our senses are frequently a distraction to our objective decision making capabilities concerning our path to Heaven. We make many choices each day to satisfy our senses, at times in contrast to a choice that would have been better for our journey. **Dying to self hurts! Sacrificial love hurts!** Imagine the sights, smells, taste, and sound of the daily life of Mother Theresa as she served the depths of humanity in the sewers of Calcutta, India. Even when given the option, she chose a simple pallet to sleep on the floor rather than personal comfort. Why? To embrace her cross. To minimize the need to satisfy her senses. To become strong in mind and stronger in heart. Frankly, if I was present in her position in my weak state, I would likely run for my life. I often make the choice of self before sacrifice. So many days I would rather veg on the couch than sacrifice my time for my children. How often the very last thing I feel like doing is serving others. I frequently fail in weakness to my senses. I fail at serving the breath of God in others. Thank God for the Cross! Thank God for the mercy of others.

I have been asked if I thought we would experience our senses in Heaven at all, or if our will would be free of them. I prayed about it and have heard many near-death experiences and it seems to me that in Heaven, our senses will be far more acute. It will be like a color blind person seeing real color for the first time. The reason why there is a difference between the senses we experience now and the senses we will experience in Heaven is that when we are in Heaven, our free-will has reached its fulfillment; which is eternity with God. Our present senses are not as acute as they were initially intended by God due to our fallen nature that our sin caused. One of the kindnesses that God has brought out of this curse is that dulled senses keep us from hurting others as badly as if our senses were super sharp.

The second point regarding suffering is that God chose to become *man* in the person of Jesus Christ. As a man, He willingly experienced and endured all forms of suffering and temptation that man experiences. He knows what we go through because He has gone through it Himself.

Third, although suffering is a reality that God allows, He uses the occasions of suffering *to benefit us* in our journey with Him and to Him. A sword must go through the fire of the kiln before it becomes a sword. It is this third point where the Lord has taught me the most.

One day I had an older couple in my office. In conversation, I quickly became aware that the woman had Alzheimer's disease. Her husband cared for her, loved her, and protected her. She didn't even know his name. "In sickness and in health . . ." This man's oath, his covenant to his wife meant something.

Later I asked the Lord, "Why do you allow Alzheimer's to exist? In essence the meaning of her life, the moment in time here on Earth for her to make the choice for God is over. Why would you continue to allow her to live?"

A short time after I asked the question, I was listening to Fr. Spitzer, President of Gonzaga University, speak on EWTN. The answer came through him in the form of the following story I summarized for you here:

> One day, 80 people were invited to a banquet. As they sat there, taking in the wonderful sights and aromas of their favorite food, they attempted to eat. Upon doing so, they discovered they were built without wrists and elbows. This realization caused wailing and gnashing of teeth as they were within inches of their favorite food, yet they could not feed themselves.
>
> The first 20 people surmised, 'There must not be a God, because if there was, He would have built us with wrists and elbows.'
>
> The second group of 20 replied, 'Well, the table is here, we are here, and we are not God, so He must exist. He must not be all powerful because if He was, He certainly would have made us with wrists and elbows.'
>
> The third group of 20 stated 'God being God, He would be omnipotent; He would be all powerful. Therefore, He must not be a *loving* God if He created us without wrists and elbows.'
>
> The fourth group of 20 looked at the others at the table in dismay, picked up their plates and leaned over the table to feed those across from themselves.
>
> This fourth group of 20 realized they were built without wrists and elbows on purpose. They found they could never truly understand unconditional love if they only fed themselves throughout time. In sharing of themselves, in giving of their lives, in carrying that cross, only then could they experience sacrificial love: the deepest kind of love.

God allows Alzheimer's not for the spiritual benefit of the individual who has the disease. He allows the situation to exist to give the rest of us the chance to "feed her." In serving her, we receive grace and virtue, virtue that would otherwise be very difficult to obtain; virtue comprised of humility, patience, fortitude, compassion, wisdom, hope, and understanding. Serving her puts each person who encounters her into a spiritual 'boot camp' of sorts, molding the caregiver's soul and preparing it for eternal life with God. The woman's Alzheimer's illness may very well have saved her husband's soul and was therefore an eternal gift to him from God.

We will all suffer. Most of us will be cognitive through it. We will be acutely aware of our pain. This means that we will all have our chance to be like Jesus and carry a cross. He did not state, "I am carrying this cross so you don't have to carry one." Rather, Jesus challenges us to "Pick up *your* cross and follow me!" (Mt16:24) We will all have the chance to gain virtue through our suffering. Through suffering, we have the opportunity to be like Christ in all ways as we can offer our suffering to God for grace and intercession for others, including the souls of purgatory. We will all experience humility in allowing others to care for us.

It is interesting how we were created. We are born into the world as infants, totally dependent on others to care for us. We depend on our parents to feed us, clothe us, change our diapers, and keep us safe. We then grow into adults and often forget that "There is a God and I am not Him." We think we are God and mistakenly think we can control everything. We live life in utter pride. We then get older and our minds and bodies start falling apart. As we start losing our ability to move, hear, see, remember, eat, breathe, and ultimately wipe our own behind, we begin to quickly realize maybe we weren't God all along. Just maybe He was caring for us this whole time! It is during this end of life experience when many find God for the first time through experiencing *humility*.

That is why euthanasia is so abhorred by the Church. It is through the crosses we all experience at the end of our lives and the associated growth of virtue that we, and those around us, inevitably grow spiritually. Many of us are then able to join God in Heaven. In many ways, we can suffer purgatory here on Earth. I am not saying we need to have a tug of war with God and stay alive at all costs. If someone has a terminal illness, there is nothing wrong with allowing nature to take its course. John Paul II did not choose to go back onto the ventilator at the end of his time here on Earth. Rather, he chose to die as naturally as possible and continued on his journey to join God.

The important issue I am addressing is the purposeful, intentional killing of someone, to "end their suffering." This includes intentionally injecting the infirmed with lethal drugs. This killing includes the failure to maintain basic life support, such as food and water. Just as all healthy people will die if we were to turn the temperature of the hospital room up to 150 degrees, all healthy people will die without food and water. Cases in which feeding tubes are removed *and* sources of nutrition are withheld are murder (for example, the Terri Shiavo case where a woman became mentally handicapped following a car accident. She had a supportive family that wanted to care for her, yet her husband intentionally starved his wife to death as he felt she would rather be dead than be handicapped).

We must instead serve those who are suffering. As the women served Christ on his journey with the cross, we are all called to serve each other when we are carrying our crosses. As in the case of the husband gaining in virtue for taking care of his wife with Alzheimer's, we too can grow in virtue when we serve one other. However, this does not mean that I have to *like* suffering; this does not mean I have to enjoy serving those who are suffering; this does not mean that I look for suffering; this does not mean that I do not fear suffering.

The good news is that I am in good company. Even Christ, during the agony in the garden the night before His death, asked God the Father to "Take this cup from me."(Mt 26:39) Like Christ, when I am suffering, I frequently ask the Father to ease my pain. Like Jesus, I also then pray that I have the strength and courage to state, "Thy will be done."

In being Catholic, I have found that the journey with Christ to the resurrection and eternal bliss must first include a journey with the cross. Being Catholic does not make me immune from suffering. If anything, the Lord is making me more and more aware of those who need to be fed, calling me to serve more and more people that I would have formerly overlooked as I am so frequently wrapped up in myself and my own needs.

If I know that I can use my crosses in life as Christ used His—for virtue for myself and grace for all mankind—then even in suffering I can still experience peace and joy. I remind myself that there are no such things as accidents. I have a choice at the moment of suffering: to wail and gnash my teeth, or to offer it up like Jesus for mercy and grace. I just think of the martyrs that were singing praise to God as they were burned alive or torn apart by the lions of the Coliseum. I think of St. Maximilian Kolbe who was joyful during his torture and death at a concentration camp during World War II. It is through the courageous and graceful acceptance of suffering by these martyrs that the observers of these events came to know God and were converted to Catholicism.

God puts all sorts of challenges in front of us on a daily basis. He gives us so many opportunities to choose Him. Most of the challenges and suffering I experience involves other people. What really helps me try to emulate Jesus, especially when I would otherwise try to run from the situation, is to look at the person I am trying to avoid as *Him*; to truly see God's breath and life in that person. An example of this would be at my workplace. I often have patients in the hospital that present as cesspools of stench, secretions, fungus, and excoriated skin who are rotting from a cancer or who are not fully cleaned for a week after using the commode. Believe me, most of the time I would rather be anywhere else but there with that patient. I would rather get out of there for the sake of my comfort and to satisfy my senses while finding a way to distract myself in order to ignore their reality.

I then ask myself, "Would I run away from Christ as He was carrying His cross? Would I run from His filthy body as he was covered in blood and dust from repeatedly falling on His journey to His crucifixion? Would I run away from His bad breath and stench of blood and death? Would I be able to look upon his beaten face, bruised and covered in blood from His crown of thorns? Would I be willing to interrupt my day, even in the uncomfortable heat of Jerusalem, and help Christ with His cross on that journey?" If I remember to look at my patients as Him, I receive the grace I need to dive into the trenches of life.

I have a much harder time finding Christ in mean, annoying, or obnoxious people. Still, I have found that, with the right perspective, the Lord allows us to grow through the daily challenges of dealing with these people by growing in virtues such as compassion, patience, fortitude, judgment, and charity. I fondly call these people "Saint-makers" because without the crosses they have bestowed upon me, I don't believe I would be in the place the Lord desires me to be at this time. So, in essence, *I have to thank the Lord for putting repulsive people into my life.* I often wonder to whom I give crosses. I must "Saint-make" a lot. If you happen to be one of those people who have received the gift of my many personality flaws, know that I pray for you to have the patience to deal with me.

I have found that there are generally two reactions to bringing the light of Christ to people who are in a state of emotional, mental, and spiritual darkness. They will either see the light as it is and gravitate toward it, changing their life forever; or they are blinded by the light and lash out at the light blaspheming the Lord and all that is good. That is when I "shake the dust from my feet" (Mk16:11) and move on. Their *reaction* to the Truth is not my responsibility. My responsibility is to try to *be Jesus* to them, to choose at that moment to obey God's request of me. If they want to crucify me for that, so be it.

At the end of the day, I realize that I do not carry my crosses in vain. I also do not carry them alone. Jesus Himself helps me with my burden. It is He who "makes my burden light."(Mt11:30) As I carry my cross to the finish line, myriads of Angels and Saints are cheering me on. They intercede for me to have the strength. They pray that I will endure. I hope that one day, with their help, I will experience *my* resurrection. I yearn for the day when I can stand in front of God and hear from the Father, "Well done my good and faithful servant . . . welcome home!" (Mt 25:23)

MARRIAGE

THE FIRST DAY I DIED to the "Religion of Self" in my life was the first day I decided that I love God and that I love my wife. I was in the ninth grade. Up to that point, every motivation I had in my life was for self. I studied hard in school so I could grow in wealth and power without working very hard. I played sports so I could attract women. I saved my money from hard work so I could buy myself a college education . . . so I could make more money. I played the piano and sang for attention. I would even do foolish things for attention. I cared purely and ultimately for self, self, self. I believed one day I would ultimately get married but that was not my problem at the time, so I did not care.

I certainly did not have a personal relationship with God. My relationship with God was completely abstract. I felt because He was forgiving, I could really do anything and it did not really matter. Heaven was a guarantee because I did not kill anybody . . . right?

I started to understand that although God loves me, in order to *receive* the gift of His love, I needed a relationship with Him. It was then that *everything* about my motivations changed. As I started to *give my life to Him*, I started to open myself to the relationship vocation He had in store for me since the time of my creation. Through prayer, I found that I longed to share everything about myself to a woman in marriage. I **started to love this woman, and I did not even know her name.** I had no idea when I would even meet her. Regardless, every motivation I then had every day, was to prepare myself for that vocation; to prepare myself for her and my family to come.

I no longer served myself in every act of every day. In early high school, I started studying in school so I could provide for my family one day. I started playing sports so I could be at my physical best, as my body was not just my own, my body was my wife's and God's as well. I played piano and sang for His glory, so I could bring others to Him through song. The irony is that I was much better at everything when the motivation was not just about 'me.' I performed better on tests and did not mind work as much. I was much more at peace with the present.

It is with this mindset that I decided to save myself physically before marriage. Up to that point, many people tried to scare me out of extramarital sex (fornication). They would talk about pregnancy, STDs like AIDS, and other deterrents. The problem is that as they were talking to a teenager. I felt I was invincible. I felt consequences could only happen to somebody else. I also knew of people giving themselves away without obvious consequence so I thought I could get away with it as well. I have also never really operated in fear.

It was when I decided I loved my wife that waiting for marriage then made sense. As I just said, my body is God's and my wife's. Until I was married, how did I know who would be my wife? Even if I thought I loved someone, without the covenant, the commitment, the oath made and sealed through the wedding vows, how would I ever truly know that this was the spouse God created for me? Without those vows given to me by my wife, how would I truly trust her intentions? How many people have thought they met "the one" and it did not ultimately work out? The words "I promise to be good to you in good times and bad, in sickness and in health, I will love you and honor you all the days of my life" are powerful words. They are the heavenly seal on the relationship between man and woman. Those words form a *lasting* covenant.

The reality is that I have never, ever met two people, young or old, in marriage that are totally and completely in love with each other who would state to each other, "I am sooo glad you gave your body to someone else, the body meant for me since the beginning of time, to those other people before we were married. It just makes me feel so happy inside. Sleeping around was so great for our long term commitment to each other . . ." **Extramarital sex is *always* an affront to a healthy, lasting marriage!** If you have fallen in this regard, there is hope . . . Repent. Accept the grace of the Cross. None of us are immune to sin.

In preparing for marriage, I knew that **my body was built *to celebrate* the sacrament of marriage.** Yes, you heard me right . . . You are not hallucinating! Just as being present at the liturgy of the Holy Mass renews our covenant with God, the *liturgy* of the marital act is an integral part of the renewal of our marriage covenant. Liturgy is an action that 1) Glorifies God 2) Sanctifies Man and 3) Builds the "Body of Christ." The marital act glorifies God as He is present and He gives us each other in marriage as a gift. The marital act itself *bestows sacramental grace* on the couple, in other words it is healthy for a marriage and for one's spiritual well-being and therefore sanctifies man. And finally, as life can come from the act itself, it literally builds the "Body of Christ."—The marital act renews the Sacrament of Marriage—it is the physical manifestation of a spiritual reality.

> "This one, at last, is bone of my bones and flesh of my flesh.
> That is why a man leaves his father and mother and clings to
> his wife, and *the two of them become one body.*" (Gen 2:23)

In marriage, I die to myself. The love I had in ninth grade for my wife, the same love I have today, is not some euphoric, lasting feeling. It is a daily, moment by moment *decision* to love my wife. It is a decision to die to myself for something greater. It is only through the death of myself that *relationship* with my spouse can even begin. Only then can I offer her everything that I am physically through the marital act. Through the same act, she is giving everything of herself to me. Again, we are celebrating a physical manifestation of a spiritual reality by renewing the Sacrament of Marriage. **That is why the marital act belongs in marriage!**

As going to Mass frequently is healthy to receive the sacramental grace of the Eucharist, **the frequent reception of sacramental grace through renewal of our marriage covenant is healthy** and can happen very often . . . Awesome!! Thank God!! Every married guy reading this chapter just said to himself that "this is the best book I have every read!!" I have a feeling this book will be pulled out and left on the night stand, open to this page as a hope in the cure of many "headaches" or "fatigue." Oh, my poor, poor wife.

Now ladies, here is the part you have been waiting for. Death to self in marriage is not just experienced physically in the bedroom (or for the more adventurous, elsewhere . . .). Death to self is an attitude that works in *every* aspect of married life, whether it is working at a job to make money to provide, caring for the children, making meals, doing dishes, cutting the lawn, driving children everywhere, and so forth. Half the time, I feel like I would die for my spouse and my family, just don't ask me to get off the couch to empty the trash . . . If a woman can get over her "headache," a guy can get over moments of weakness as well.

Now some reading this will say to themselves, "I thought this guy was Catholic. He seems to be surprisingly casual about discussing his love life in marriage." The truth is that physical love in marriage is a great gift from God. **It is not some side-effect of creation that God 'tolerates' for the propagation of our species.** It is not like I praise God at every moment in my life and somehow try to hide from Him when I am celebrating my marriage with my wife. If anything, He is likely there at that moment more than most, as we are vulnerable through the giving of ourselves.

There is a distorted sexual philosophy where one should be ashamed of and embarrassed by marital love as was described well by Dr. Gregory Popcak when he described the disordered "Aunt Mcgillicuddy's Urn School of Sexuality."

> "It grudgingly admits that sex is beautiful—in a grotesque, overdone, gothic sort of way—but above all, sex is holy and therefore, a little like Aunt Mcgillicuddy's antique urn; it must be approached delicately, cautiously, and (ideally) infrequently. That is, 'We oonly tooch it if we have to dust it, and then, oonly once a month or soo.'"

Meanwhile, Satan has taken the great gift of marital love, and twisted it into an act of selfishness when it is not in the context of marriage. This distortion is what permeates most perceptions of sex. When holy people ascribe to Aunt Mcgillicuddy's guarded style, many people, especially teens, are never exposed to the holy *celebration and gift* that marital love represents. The truth is that marital love was the first commandment ordered by God Himself: "Be fertile and multiply; fill the earth and subdue it." (Gen 1:28) Yes folks, in the context of marriage,

God is *commanding* us to go and have a good time with each other. Why should we be ashamed of or embarrassed by God's command and gift to us? Ultimately, we who clearly understand the *celebration* that marital love represents, need to stop tiptoeing around and stand out more publically as a healthy contrast to Satan's distorted, selfish model of human sexuality.

As Elizabeth and I die to ourselves in marriage, *we are simultaneously opening our "one body" to the presence of God in our lives and our marriage.* Our marriage becomes holy. **With the openness to the presence of God comes openness to life because God is Life.**

As God the Father eternally loves God the Son, God the Holy Spirit "proceeds" from that relationship. Therein lays the mystery of the Trinity. **Life is manifest in love as God is Life and God is Love. Creation and life is God just being God.**

Similarly, children given as gifts to parents are the walking, talking manifestation of the love the spouses have for each other. Repeatedly, throughout scripture, God's greatest gift to His faithful was the gift of children. Children are the fruit of love. Children are the reward to death to self and total self-giving in marriage. In our death to self, life is born. That is the principle of why Catholic couples should always be open to life and not use artificial contraception.

Artificial contraception is an affront to giving of ourselves totally and completely. It therefore has no place in marriage. It would be like telling my wife, "I offer all of myself to you, except my fertility." In having kids, parents have the opportunity to experience God in a different perspective because to our kids, we are god. Meanwhile, there are no beings on earth closer to God the Father than children. Kids are the way we once were before we "ate the apple." Total trust. Total innocence. "Whoever humbles himself like this child is the greatest in the Kingdom of Heaven."(Mt18:4)

There have been times in my marriage where we were on the brink of total exhaustion. The life of my family moves at high speed. We work hard and have many small children. In those times, my wife and I were able to exercise some self-control while using Natural Family Planning. God gave woman a neat cycle where there are times in the month she is far more likely to conceive than others. There is nothing about God's plan regarding marriage where every time the marriage vows are renewed, the couple is *trying* to conceive. That said, every couple at all times in marriage should be *open to the possibility to life*. They should be open to the God's will and receive the gift of children when the opportunity presents itself.

Natural Family Planning fosters communication which deepens a marital relationship. Although the national average for divorce is over 50%, the average divorce rate for those using Natural Family Planning is 0.2%. Obviously, Natural Family Planning is one piece of a larger puzzle on why these relationships last, but the correlation is so stark that it cannot be ignored.

Some argue that using *Natural* Family Planning instead of *artificial* contraception is just splitting hairs. The difference is in the names I just highlighted. God made a woman's body to behave in a natural cycle that is also used when a couple is *trying* to conceive. Nothing, in both cases of Natural Family Planning whether Natural Family Planning is used with a couple trying to conceive or not, is withheld within the marital act itself. The chips then fall where *God* wills.

Artificial contraception is man, through the "Religion of Self," intentionally creating barriers to life. Artificial contraception is man therefore creating barriers to God, as God is Life.

Marriage is a covenant. Covenants are a lasting promise. If my wife chose to not want to stay with me in marriage, it would pull apart the very fabric of my being and I would die as the man that I am because I am her and she is me. The vows establishing covenant in marriage is why divorce is not allowed in the Catholic Church and condemned by God.

> "Some Pharisees approached him, and tested him saying, 'Is it lawful for a man to divorce his wife for *any* cause whatever?' He (Jesus) said in reply, 'Have you not read that from the beginning the Creator 'made them male and female' and said, 'For this reason a man shall leave his father and mother and be joined to his wife, and the two shall become one flesh?' So they are no longer two, but one flesh. Therefore, what God has joined together, no human must separate."(Mt 19:3)

Jesus spoke against divorce in all four Gospels. He was not vague about this topic at all. That said, a couple maintains individual free-wills in marriage and sadly, can choose not to love the other, or to ultimately die to themself. Therefore, although a Catholic marriage remains valid, the couple does not need to live together and can become separated, especially if abuse is present. The Catholic Church would strongly encourage a couple to attempt reconciliation, even in cases of infidelity. Ultimately a civil (legal) divorce for the separation of property may be needed, yet spiritually, a married couple is still married, whether they live together or not because marriage is covenant. Therefore separated Catholics are not to remarry if they hope to remain "in God's grace."

> "Whoever divorces his wife (unless the marriage is unlawful) causes her to commit adultery, and whoever marries a divorced woman commits adultery. Again you have heard that it was said to your ancestors, 'Do not take a false oath, but make good to the Lord all that you vow.'"(Mt 5:32)

Yes, the teaching on divorce is a tough teaching but it is true. It is tough, as the call to perfection and Sainthood is also tough.

Again, in the "Religion of Self," marriage is typically avoided at all costs because successful marriage promotes death to self. In the "Religion of Self" children are an absolute threat and burden. In the "Religion of Self," relationship and the community of the family is *anathema*. Hence, in a world of "self," extra-marital sex has become the norm. Abortion is perceived to be needed. And in the world of "self," the very concept on marriage is therefore under attack.

Because the "Religion of Self" is so deeply rooted in our culture, when people are getting married after years of extramarital relationships and co-habitation where they pretend they are married, it frequently ends in divorce. Why? Because the "Religion of Self" is brought into the marriage. These couples are used to leaving *pretend* marriages repeatedly before actually marrying. Why would that habit of leaving when challenges arise, magically disappear when one finally ties the knot in marriage, especially if they are still living for self? In marrying a spouse who had a similar pre-marriage experience, real trust would be hard to establish because there would always seem to be one foot out the door. It is like playing a game of "chicken" with their spouse because one would always maintain an emotional wall, not offering too much of themself in the fear that the pain would be that much worse if the relationship ended as so many prior relationships had ended.

As marriages are ending at an alarming rate, the children of these unions are often left without a stable, parental upbringing by both a mother *and* a father. Kids are simple. They do not need money. They need safety and love. They also significantly benefit by being raised by *both* a mother and a father. In some situations where the child's safety is threatened or there is no love present, being raised by a single parent may be necessary but it is most definitely NOT the ideal. "It takes a village to raise a child" is total nonsense. Since the first existence of man, it takes only a mother and father.

As the family unit is crumbling under the "Religion of Self," and we have a generation raised by "the village," the normal family unit led by mom and dad is therefore questioned as even necessary. That is why there is a mass, organized, systematic push to normalize gay 'marriage.' The homosexual revolution has clearly taken notice of the weakness of "traditional marriage," and is using this opportunity to *normalize* disorder. Most young people in this new generation have no concept of what a normal family is, and therefore why not let everybody 'marry' anything?

Let's clear the air for a moment. If you haven't noticed, I am a fairly blunt guy. I truly love those who suffer from same sex attraction. Jesus loves them too. If he were walking the earth today, those are the people who he would spend a lot of time with. The Catholic Church loves those with same sex attraction. They are our brothers and sisters. The Catholic Church has therefore set up support groups for those with same sex attraction like "Courage." We should never discriminate against them in any way. Yet, we should not encourage our brothers and sisters to *act* in sin either. Same sex attraction *is a disorder*. If it wasn't and was the order of creation, we would not exist. Let me tell you a secret . . . We are all disordered!! Some people have a tendency to lie. Others have an inclination to gossip. Yet others struggle with the disorders of gluttony, anorexia, fornication, or alcoholism. Others have more serious disorders like pedophilia. Same sex attraction is therefore not *license to sin*, to act upon those disordered instincts.

> "Let the one among you who is without sin be the first to throw a stone at her"... "Woman, where are they? Has no one condemned you?... Neither do I condemn you. Go, *and from now on do not sin anymore.*"(Jn8:7)

The Catholic Church has always promoted self-control, self-physical mastery. This includes self-control in marriage. This includes self-control for the clergy and for those who are single. Why is there a call for an exemption with those of same sex attraction? We are not animals. Human beings can make conscious decisions that defy animal instincts. That consciousness is what differ us humans from animals. Again, this is a hard reality for some. The reality is that those with same sex attraction are called to single life. They are called to love others *as we are all called* to love others. Like all others who are not married, they are called to physical self-control.

All the principles discussed in this chapter also apply to vocations of those who are single and those called to the religious life. Single life is most definitely not an "inferior" vocation to marriage. In fact it is quite the opposite. St. Paul stated it accurately, "It is better to be single, only proceed with marriage if you must."(1Cor7:27) I did not understand that statement until I got married. Before I was married, the Lord would say "jump" and I would ask "how high?" Since marriage, the Lord says "jump" and I turn to my wife and ask "Honey, how high are *we* going to jump?"

Those called to the vocation of single consecrated life or religious life need to also die to themselves and give themselves totally and completely to their 'spouse,' who is God. For a priest, he serves his spouse by serving his parish. For a single person, they serve their spouse by serving the community at large.

Lord, I pray that we can find the vocation you have set forth for us in our life. I pray that we can die to ourselves so we can be open to your will. In our vocation, help us further to die to ourselves so we can serve each other. I pray to be a good husband and father. Mold me into the man you expect me to be. I am yours.

MISDIRECTED COMPASSION

One day, on a television show on EWTN, there was a priest in a room surrounded by several young people. These young adults were peppering the priest with question after question. The questions concerned the contemporary social "norms" about which the group thought the Church to be "out of touch." They questioned why the Church opposes gay marriage, contraception, extramarital sex, abortion, woman being priests, stem cell research, euthanasia, in vitro fertilization, missing Mass, and boyfriend/girlfriend co-habitation before marriage. These questions were intermixed with their stated opinion that the "Catholic Church has outdated views of society."

The priest stood there and absorbed what seemed like an eternity of questioning, almost like he was on the witness stand in a courtroom. The aggressive young people didn't seem to be interested in his initial answers to their questions. They continued asking the next question before he finished answering the prior question. He ultimately stopped responding to the verbal attacks, leaned back, and smiled. The commotion died down. Then the priest spoke.

"Has God Changed?" Bam! Then there was silence. These young adults got it. If God is Truth, the Truth does not change. God doesn't respond to opinion polls. The Truth doesn't change if a majority of people ignore it. The Truth doesn't change over time. *God* is the same today as He was yesterday and as He will be tomorrow. *Truth* is the same today as it was yesterday and as it will be tomorrow. **Again, there is nothing less relevant to the Truth and Reality of the universe than**

our personal opinion! Needless to say, no one in the crowd had any courage to ask him any more questions.

God is Truth. Meanwhile, Satan is referred to in scripture as the "Father of Lies."(Jn8:44) What he often does is twist a person's natural desire to do virtuous acts and directs that effort to ultimately serve him and his purposes. He is an expert in convincing us weak and unguarded humans to unwittingly join him in doing evil. One of his more subtle techniques is to take a person's natural feeling of compassion and misdirect it.

Our society unknowingly supports sin because we have *misdirected compassion*. We have compassion for the individuals called to self-control and physical-mastery. That is why we don't dare to encourage people to refrain from sex until marriage and until, as a married couple, they are open to life. We have compassion for those with same sex attraction so we turn a blind eye to unnatural and sinful behavior. We have compassion for the woman who is choosing to terminate her child in an abortion. We have compassion for the couple who cannot conceive so we don't speak of the immorality of unnatural conception. We have compassion for the handicapped, so if the handicapped person is unborn, we 'compassionately' kill them through abortion. We have compassion for the physically ill, so we kill healthy unborn children for their cells to use in embryonic stem cell research. We have compassion for those who physically or mentally suffer, so we compassionately kill them through euthanasia. In the name of 'compassion,' Satan has slowly guided us in *justifying* the "Religion of Self" for ourselves.

Our society is missing a major rule of basic morality. **The end does NOT justify the means!** In other words, even if we could cure humanity of the horrible disease of cancer by killing only one innocent, unwilling person, it is never moral to proceed. If our end is to reduce suffering by intentionally killing those who suffer, that is never moral. If we allow a woman to "pursue happiness", but in doing so she is massacring her children, that is never moral.

"Tolerance" of sin and evil has never been, nor should ever be, a Catholic virtue. Catholics are called to practice *charity to those in sin*. In the end, we are all sinners (especially me). We all have weaknesses. We all have crosses to carry. I have compassion for everyone in their weakness. That does not mean that I want to ever condone or even be apathetic to sin.

The reason why sin and evil are flourishing in our society is <u>not</u> because evil has somehow become stronger than it used to be. **It is through the apathy about sin by good people that sin has taken a stronghold in today's world.** Satan has caused good people to become confused. He often convinces good, holy people to avoid standing up for the Truth for fear of being hypocrites. Through this fear, Satan then acts in our society unopposed. Society then tolerates a moral code which is based upon the least common denominator of human decency.

The truth is: **we are all hypocrites!** The only non-hypocrites that have ever walked the earth are Jesus Christ and the Virgin Mary. Just because we are sinners does not mean that we should not strive to be better in mind and deed. Just because we are weak, we should not lower the "moral bar" of our society to our present state of weakness.

Likewise, we are admonished by the "politically correct" proponents, "Do not judge others!" It is true that we should not judge whether others are going to Hell. Rather, we should have mercy on all who are in error and encourage them to "sin no more." However, Satan has twisted our thinking about judging *people's souls* (predicting whether they are going to heaven or hell) versus judging an *action* as good or evil.

The result of this twisted thinking and rampant confusion is that the discernment between good and evil has become a social taboo. The Truth is: **we must judge *actions* as good or evil.** If we are aware that an action is evil and sinful due to the teaching and example of Christ, then we know it is damaging to the soul. It is like a spiritual cancer. If we love others in our society, we have a responsibility to educate them on the difference between healthy behavior and unhealthy behavior. If we know the stove is hot, we must tell others before they touch it. We cannot sit idly by and allow sin to become our cultural 'norm.' In this case, to do nothing—to be apathetic—is to sin! *True compassion* for others will lead us to show them the path to Heaven, not to sit by and idly allow sin to enslave them!

Stand up! Stand up for the Truth! Stand up for all that is good! Be a light in this time of darkness! Stand up for our Lord! Stand up for our Master! Stand up for our King!

LIFE

SHE IS IN THE EIGHTH grade. She looks like an angel from heaven. In her early childhood she had blond ringlets that would have made Shirley Temple jealous. She has almond brown eyes that are the doorway to her soul. She enjoys boys and her circle of girlfriends. She gets straight A's in school (quietly) and is mature beyond her years. She loves to paint and draw. She enjoys softball and surfing. She loves her dog and her parents. She would say she has had a great life. She has dreams of her future and has ambition and goals. She is loved by all who encounter her. She is the kind of young lady that would seek out and befriend the new kid in class, not because she lacked friends, but because it is her nature. She is the joy of so many that have had the privilege to know her. Some day she will make a man very happy in marriage. They will have children of their own and grandchildren and great-grandchildren. It is through this life of hers that generations of lives will inherit such goodness, such peace and love. This great life, this fantastic person was a hairs-breadth from an early death.

Life simply cannot be imagined if she were not here. All who have encountered this young lady would not have experienced how bright and wonderful this life on Earth can be if she was not a part of it.

Meanwhile, the mother-to-be of this young lady grew up in a culture which bombarded her with values contrary to Catholic teaching. As her own value system formed, she came to believe that sexual intimacy was to be reserved until you found someone "you love." However, there was never an expectation of holding onto that gift until reaching the commitment of marriage. As a result, at age 16, this teenager gave herself for the first time to her boyfriend of several years. She happened to be fertile and thus became pregnant.

When she first became aware of her situation, she told her boyfriend and his parents. They immediately went into a state of denial. They simply refused to accept that reality. They just hoped the situation would disappear. They wouldn't allow their son to speak to her or associate with her in any way. The boyfriend's parents and her boyfriend simply abandoned her in her time of need.

Meanwhile, something had to be done. There was the obvious problem: this 16 year-old, pregnant teenager was afraid to tell her parents. She was fearful that they would never understand. What if they rejected her also? What if they kicked her out of the house? She felt completely alone.

Desperate thoughts filled her mind. She knew there was a way out. All she had to do was have an abortion. No one would know. It would solve all of her problems. She could continue life like nothing had happened.

Then God intervened. Grace abounded. Truth kissed her. Suddenly she was enlightened and saw the problem clearly. If she had an abortion, *she* would know; *God* would know. She could never escape herself. She would never be able to look herself in the eye again. Her maternal instinct screamed to her that if she were to destroy the child inside her, she would be destroying a part of her own soul.

She waited until her father was not around before she told her mother. Her mother was supportive. Together they decided to tell her father when he was away on business and thousands of miles away from home. Distance would be a protective buffer.

They called her father. Much to their surprise, there was no explosion. There were no threats. The father immediately began to help. Inspired by the Spirit, he contacted his married brother. His brother and his brother's wife had wanted children for years but could not have them naturally. This was an answer to their prayers!

The pregnant teenager was invited to live with her aunt and uncle during the ensuing months. Finally the teenage mother gave birth to her beautiful, baby girl who was then immediately adopted by the mother's aunt and uncle. It is through this "bad" situation that tremendous goodness was released into the world. Although the child was initially unintended by this couple, this child was *not* unintended by God. This young teenage girl gave her aunt and uncle the love of their lives. The child has, and hopefully will continue to have, a great life. The teenage mother faced adversity and, with God's grace, triumphed. In delivering that child, the teenage mother for the first time in her life realized that God is *real*! In carrying her cross, she *experienced* God's love for her. She died to herself and became resurrected into a woman of honor, character, dignity, and strength. In her fall, with her determination to get back up, she understood her call to be a saint. She was being molded by God for her true love in her marriage to come. She was being prepared for her soul-mate. She was being prepared to become *my wife*. There are no accidents.

The fateful day my wife chose to allow her child to live, over 2,200 women in the United States faced that same decision and made a tragic mistake. Undoubtedly most of these women are good people, perhaps even holy people. But in their moment of distress, in their moment of abandonment, they are "helped" by parents, doctors, and friends who have bought into the biggest lie of our age. These misguided helpers with their *misdirected compassion*, these unwitting accomplices to the "Father of Lies", convince these young pregnant women to abort their own babies. After all, they argue, it is the "right" of the mother to terminate her pregnancy. The unborn baby has no rights. The unborn baby has not yet achieved 'personhood'; the unborn baby is really only a fetus. It is only a very small, unimportant glob of tissue.

We must all seek the Truth in this issue. Too much is at stake to put our heads in the sand and pretend that there is not a problem. It helps if we realize that "There is a God and I am not Him." It helps if we are willing to spend a few minutes and reflect with openness. Think about it. Society must acknowledge that the unborn are genetically human. Human women do not deliver dogs or elephants or carrots or fish. Society must also agree that the unborn entity is "alive." Unborn people, like born people, are composed of cells that are growing, reproducing, metabolizing, developing and living.

Our society and justice system made a law in Roe vs. Wade that doesn't allow that unborn, human, alive, child to achieve 'personhood' until the unborn child has fully passed through some invisible magical force-field in the birth canal. Without personhood, even though the unborn child is alive and human, the unborn child is not protected under our laws.

It is therefore fully legal to experiment on the child or use that child's nervous system as spare parts for the handicapped in "embryonic stem cell research." It is also fully legal to burn the skin off of this unborn child with chemicals until they bleed to death, dismember this child by sharp surgical instruments, and eviscerate this child through high powered suction and blending. It is even legal during delivery to stab a partially born child in the back of the skull and remove the child's brains while the child is still in the birth canal and collapse her skull. This "partial birth abortion" is legal as long as a portion of the child's body remains in the mother. Five seconds later, when the child is completely outside the birth canal, stabbing the child is considered murder. *Have we completely lost our minds?*

Legal abortion is not the first time that genocide was justified by denying the personhood of alive, human beings. Hitler justified the Holocaust because the Jews were not classified as 'persons' under German law. Our United States Supreme Court justified slavery through the "Dred Scott Decision" whereby African-Americans were not given 'personhood' and were therefore enslaved like livestock. There has never been a time in human history when mankind has been correct when separating the status of 'personhood' from alive, human beings.

That is why the Catholic Church, long before our Declaration of Independence, identified all human beings as having the inalienable rights of "life, liberty, and the pursuit of happiness." Inalienable rights are rights that we don't have to earn. They are rights that are inherent to us because we *exist* and because of our respect for human life and human dignity. The most basic of these rights is the *right to life* because, without it, all other rights are irrelevant. If you are dead, your other rights are of little value.

Ironically, the 'personhood' of the child in modern culture is based solely on whether or not the mother *wants* the child to be a person. The unborn child is protected under the laws *if* the mother wants to 'keep her baby.' For example, if a pregnant woman is murdered, the murderer gets charged with two counts of murder. What is unbelievable about this is that the mother can, at any time, go and kill that child in an abortion and our society will subsidize that abortion through Planned Parenthood. Does this make any sense to anybody?

If a mother looks at her child and decides that she does not want her child to be a person anymore, does that child objectively cease to be a child? If that same woman looked at a tree and declared that it was not a tree, does the tree objectively cease to be a tree? Why do different principles apply to the unborn?

At what stage of development does the unborn child become a person? The pro-abortionist would argue that at any time during the nine months before birth the unborn child "has not yet developed into a human-being." They would claim that in the first few weeks and months of life the unborn child is "just a few cells."

My retort is that that child is *supposed* to be a few cells at that age. I have five children. My 2 year old doesn't look like my three-year-old who doesn't look like my six-year-old who doesn't look like my 10-year-old who doesn't look like my twelve-year-old. They are all still developing and will be until death. This development started at conception. Genetically, everything you are right now was present at that first cell. *Life did not begin after the child passed through the magical, invisible force field in the birth canal.* A one-day-old, unborn, one-celled child is supposed to go through that normal stage of human development. This logic is also true of a more developed three-week-old unborn child and an even more developed eight-month-old. That is normal human development. Everyone reading this chapter was once a one-celled unborn child that continued growing *before* and *after* birth. In short, the act of birth did not cause development to cease. Therefore, the argument that the child isn't "developed" is not applicable.

If 'personhood' is to be assigned at some random moment of development, what happened in that moment of time that justifies that conclusion? For example, if 'the line' is at 3 months for the unborn, is the child truly not the same at 2 months, 29 days, 23hrs and 59 minutes? Of course the child is the same! The moment is arbitrary. If you were to ask, "What is the difference in a child as we go back in time, second by second?" the answer is the same. Nothing! You would find yourself having to start at conception to assign the title of personhood.

Some argue for abortion by saying that the child might be "born into a poor environment." If abortion is compassionate for the poor, why discriminate? The same principle should be applied to all the poor and we should then be 'compassionately' eliminating everybody we consider to be poor.

Some argue that the child might be handicapped. If that is the principle, we should consider 'compassionately' killing all those who have handicaps now. In short, for whatever 'compassionate' reason abortion is justified, the same principle should then apply to those of us fortunate enough to have passed through the magical, invisible force-field of the birth canal.

Every time my wife is pregnant, we hear the comment from good hearted people: "as long as the baby is healthy . . ." I have always thought to myself, "and if they are not?" There are no guarantees in life. My children might get into a car accident or become ill at any time. Would I be expected to abort them then?

Some people are confused because abortion has been made legal. They have unwittingly fallen into the moral trap that "since an act is legal, it is therefore moral." If our great democracy voted to make rape legal, would it then be moral? Should we not have a law against rape, even if some are going to break the law and rape women anyway?

Many focus on the 7% of abortions done for medical reasons or rape and incest and therefore turn a blind eye to the other 93% of abortions done strictly with the mindset of birth control.

In regards to rape and incest, abortions done for these reasons are about 1%. Studies have proven that when a woman has an abortion after a rape, she still suffers from post-abortion syndrome. In many ways, having that abortion is like allowing that rapist to control her again. The child also didn't ask to be there. If the child of the rapist was born and standing in front of us, could we justify killing the child then? There are many families that would be more than willing to adopt that child and, in a way, the mother of that child could live the rest of her life knowing the rapist didn't turn *her* into a murderer. In the end she defeated evil and turned a negative situation into a positive one.

Consider the mother that has an abortion for medical reasons. The Catholic Church is clear in this situation. If the mother's *life* is in jeopardy during a pregnancy, *her* life is not less valuable than the life of her child. The effort should then to be to save *both* the mother and child, even if that means delivering the child early and doing our best to save that child. This approach holds even if the odds of rescue are slim. We should still give the child a chance at pulling through. If there was an avalanche that buried skiers, we would still search for them even if the odds of survival are low and the path treacherous. If the mother had cancer and needed chemotherapy which would be harmful to the unborn child, it would still be permissible as her intention would be to treat the cancer, not to harm her child.

The same reasoning applies to the treatment of an ectopic pregnancy. An ectopic pregnancy is the situation whereby an unborn child implants somewhere other than uterus, often in the fallopian tube. If that portion of the fallopian tube is not removed, *both* mother and child would die. Removal of that diseased portion of the fallopian tube is essential to prevent the same situation from occurring again. The *intention* is never to kill the child although that is the inevitable outcome. The intention should be to save the lives of both, in all circumstances, if possible. *Intention is everything.*

Pay attention to our politicians as they discuss this however. The pro-abortionists don't discuss the 'life' of the mother; they discuss the 'health' of the mother. Health has been defined by the Supreme Court in Doe vs. Bolton as "mental, psychological, emotional, or financial health." **Abortion is legal until *birth* in all states of this country if the mothers 'health' is in question.** In other words, at nine months gestation, at which time the mother could have a c-section, she can legally abort her child if she states that she is depressed or not financially 'healthy.'

In embryonic stem cell research, our country has compassion for those who are ill or handicapped. Through that 'misdirected compassion,' we are legalizing experimentation on the unborn and the use of their parts. What I would like answered by Michael J. Fox and his followers is the question: "How many children are you willing to slaughter for their parts so you don't have Parkinson's disease anymore? 1,000? 100? 10? 1?" Again, are we going to allow the ends to justify the means?

Some argue that this is a private issue and the government should stay out of it. If that same child was born and lived in the privacy of the woman's home, and the woman was burning off her child's skin or stabbing the back of the child's skull with a scissors, wouldn't the child's right to life supersede that woman's right to privacy?

What does this mean? The truth of this matter is hard to comprehend. Nearly as many children are killed *every single day* in this country than those who were killed on the 9/11/2001 Twin Tower attack in New York City. More children are killed in our country *each year* than have died in all wars America has ever fought. Nearly every fourth child conceived is aborted. More than 50,000,000 lives have been slaughtered in this contemporary American Holocaust. Why?

It all comes down to the most predominant "religion" in the United States today: *the Religion of Self.* Abortion is just a symptom of the mindset of our time. We want to live a life without consequence. This includes, of course, our sexual life. We want to have 'the freedom' to have sex with anything that breathes and not have to worry about consequences. Again, children are a perceived threat for the quest of power and control. Children are perceived by many as a burden. Our society therefore continues to ignore the blatant Truth and the magnitude of the abortion problem.

Instead of cherishing our woman and honoring them in their femininity and supporting them when they are pregnant, with abortion we destroy that which distinguishes woman from men. We attack every fiber of maternal instinct and minimize the human life growing inside of her as "just a blob of cells." In essence, we are all just a blob of cells. Abortion and embryonic stem cell research are evil. **Abortion and embryonic stem cell research are acts that are *always* rooted in selfishness.** They are wrong, every time, always . . . period. The Catholic Church defines abortion as "gravely immoral."(CCC 2272) In participating in an abortion, whether having one, advising friends or family to have an abortion, promoting the abortion cause, or intentionally voting for politicians who advance abortion in our society, one is placing on oneself a "lampshade of sin" thick enough to block out the light, that is, the life of grace given to us. We become separated from God.

As was mentioned, one fourth of pregnancies end in abortion. *Think* of how many people you know who may have had an abortion. Think of how many boyfriends and fathers and parents and friends were instrumental in encouraging that act. Perhaps one of the reasons why abortion still exists in this country is that there is a subconscious, mistaken belief that since "everyone is doing it", and we live in a democracy, we are safe from personal responsibility and the judgment of God. To correct the error it would take countless people to practice humility and have the capacity to admit making a massive mistake. Most find it simply easier to pretend nothing is wrong. It would seem that many are afraid of having participated in this level of evil, and therefore feel the urge to fight to keep the lie alive. It would be like being a German who sought out Jews to send to a concentration camp or working in the concentration camp itself and deciding later that Jews are people too. It takes a lot of courage to become self-aware.

For those who have participated in abortion, welcome to humanity in sin. We have all fallen. We all need the Cross. God is merciful. The light of God in all of our lives is always on, waiting for us to repent and remove the "lampshades" we have placed over His light. In repentance and humility, we have the ability to allow the grace of the Cross of Christ back in our lives and we can once again be set free of this great burden of sin. Jane Roe (from Roe v. Wade), whose real name is Norma McCorvey, understood this and repented. She became aware of how she was "used" by those with misdirected compassion to further their cause. That is why she became a Christian and is now a leader in the fight to end abortion. She is a hero and is now working on sainthood. She is on the path that can lead to eternity with God. Finding this path and staying on it is the goal of every saint. Every saint has entered this path at a different point in his or her life, usually found through humility and repentance.

What now? I had to first accept the gravity of the present situation, especially politically. Does it really matter if I have a perfect candidate in every other issue such as gun control, taxes, education, health care, and national defense if that candidate is for the slaughter of 2,200 children each day? Does the importance of any other issue come remotely close? Readers, please consider making the end of abortion a top priority by voting for the candidate that is most pro-life, whether that candidate is a Republican or a Democrat, or an Independent

Secondly, use your voice. Speak for the unborn as they cannot speak for themselves. Talk to anyone who will listen. Encourage uniting those looking to abort their children with the thousands upon thousands of couples flying all over the world to adopt a child because there are so few children left here at home to adopt.

Thirdly, pray. After that, pray some more. Pray for a conversion of hearts. Pray for an end to the "Religion of Self." Pray for awareness to the Truth. Pray for God to have mercy. Become a light in this time of darkness.

The good news is that, like the end of slavery and the end of the Jewish Holocaust, mankind ultimately comes to its senses. The question is: how many tens of millions of children will be slaughtered in the interim? How many souls of the living will die spiritually as a result of this atrocity? And the final question we should ask ourselves: *will I be able to look at my grandchildren in the eyes and state that I did everything in my power to stop this bloodshed?*

CAMP VERITAS

THERE HAS ALWAYS BEEN AN undercurrent of spiritual preparation and learning occurring throughout my whole life. As I entered my teen years and grew in my relationship with the Lord, I became more aware of this reality. I was being molded by the Lord. For what purpose I had yet to find out. Since then I have tried to give control of my everyday life to the Holy Spirit and in doing that, I am now convinced that **there are no accidents.** Therefore, I try to learn from every situation, whether I perceive it as good or bad, and try to identify and understand what God is trying to teach me.

The Lord is merciful. He usually only shows me the next few steps of the journey. It is like climbing a mountain in the fog. If I truly saw how large and treacherous the mountain was before I started, I probably would not have bothered trying to climb it, telling the Lord His expectations of me were impossible.

The good news is that I don't see the whole mountain; I see only the next several yards and they don't look that difficult. With that limited visibility, I find myself often doing what I would have formerly considered for me to be unlikely. For example, if you were to tell me and my English teachers in high school that I would one day be writing a book, we would have laughed out loud.

There have been many learning situations in which the Lord has taught me profound lessons. One of these lessons occurred at a point in my life when I was having a difficult time at work. I was trying to control a situation to help make our business to become more successful. The problem was that my warnings and suggestions were not always heeded. Following a tense meeting with my employers, I was totally stressed out. I started obsessively planning my next move: who I would talk to, what

I would I say, and when would I say it. As usual, when my mind got into that obsessive problem solving mode, I shut out everything else. I was distant to my family. I didn't sleep well. I was unable to focus on normal tasks at hand.

It was during this stressful time that my wife recommended that I attend daily Mass with her. She's so great. Gosh, I love her. I agreed. Upon arrival, we chose to sit in a front pew of church. Following Mass, a woman I had never met before approached me. I found out later that she is a Jewish convert to Catholicism. She said, "The Lord wants me to tell you something." I thought to myself, "Yeah, right lady," but I listened just to be polite. She continued, "The Lord wants you to know that He really loves you. He has great plans for you. Don't worry about it; He will take care of it." With those words, she gave me a hug and walked off.

Instantly the flood of thoughts turning the treadmill in my brain stopped. I could no longer even *think* about my work-related petty worries. I felt mental and emotional peace. Her statement became the motto of my life: **If the Lord loves me, what else *really* matters?** Everything else is anxiety about the false control I *think* I have when I forget that **"There is a God and I am not Him."** If I can look at that cross and truly believe God loves me, nothing else matters. My only remaining task is to fulfill the meaning of my life and choose to obey the Lord, moment by moment, in my life. I really do not have control over anything else. That inclination to obey flows from having the *trust* that the Lord knows what He is doing.

I continued to listen to the Lord and my next step up the mountain of life began to emerge from the fog. As I was sitting in Mass one day with my family, I looked around the church and found that we were the only people in the building under the age of 60. The mean age of the church community is rising. The youth are not retained following their Confirmation in eighth grade. The number of men answering the call to priesthood is dwindling. It is only a matter of time before churches are closed. Many churches will disappear, not in a hundred years or fifty years, but in the next twenty years unless something changes. The "Religion of Self" permeates deeply within the contemporary thinking of our culture. It is destroying the individual. It is destroying the family. It is therefore destroying the Church.

As I imagined standing next to my Church while the Church seemed to be on life support from this preventable disease, my heart was broken. I love God's Church. I thought, "If I don't do something about this, how can I expect anybody else to." At the time, I thought about how I came to know the Lord. It was not by going to CCD or Confirmation class for an hour a week. It was not from some great homily I heard once in church. The way I found the Lord was by spending time with the Lord in front of the Eucharist.

Imagine an Alcoholics Anonymous program that has meetings once a week for an hour. Imagine the alcoholics hearing about alcohol for the hour, however, *the alcoholic never made the decision to actually stop drinking.* The first thing the alcoholic would do, would be to go home and drink following the meeting. This would continue through the entire AA program. If the Alcoholics had an AA picnic for a day, that same alcoholic would go home and drink twice as much as usual. The only thing that is effective for most alcoholics is to go to detox for a time, a time separated from their alcohol so they can make an objective choice if they want to continue with alcohol in their life or not. Only then, once the decision has been made, does the weekly meeting at AA make sense and becomes effective.

One of the main reasons we are dying as a Church is because we are losing 90% of our teens the very week after they have been confirmed in the eighth grade. These teens went to their Confirmation classes weekly for years, heard about Christ, *yet never made the decision to actually follow him.* The Catholic Church has had its own detox for 2000 years. It is called pilgrimage. Pilgrimage is stepping out of our lives long enough that we can look back at our life and make the objective call of whether we are on a path that leads to our eternal destination of Heaven, or not. It is the time to make the decision to become *a disciple* of Jesus Christ. Only after that decision is made, does going to Mass make sense. Only then does going to Confirmation class make sense to continue to nurture that decision.

As a chubby boy at heart, I think of many things in relation to food. Imagine the Church has great barbeque sauce. Imagine the sauce is made up of the Mass, Adoration, the rosary, catechesis, and personal testimonies. Then imagine dumping that sauce all at once on some ribs.

The sauce all burns off. It does not soak in. Imagine microwaving the ribs. They taste just awful. The key to good cooking in this case is time. **The key ingredient to making disciples of Christ, is time in front of the Cross—time in front of the Eucharist.** There is nothing wrong with the recipe the Church has been using for millennia. Those running these programs have simply turned up the heat too much and the sauce is burning off. We are trying to teach the entirety of the church in some 6 hour retreat. It is simply not enough time to have these youth step out of the business of their lives to listen. It is not enough time in front of the Cross to allow the reality of the Cross to soak in and build a personal relationship with God.

Allowing the grace of the Cross to soak in also entails identifying the enemy: the "Religion of Self." It is much easier to fight a disease when you identify what the disease is. Through prayer, and finally submitting to the persistent nagging of my heart by the Lord, the solution became obvious. Stamp out the "Religion of Self"; introduce teens to their God; and invite them to drink the living water of grace found at the base of the Cross. Invite them to drink not just little sips, but to dive head-first into that font of grace!

This is where the idea of Camp Veritas came to fruition (Veritas in Latin means "Truth"). Camp Veritas would be an overnight camp where the youth of the Faith stop the business of their lives for a week and go on pilgrimage to be with the Lord. Camp Veritas would offer education about the Faith.

I found that in some parishes, the teens are taught by volunteers that are usually not comfortable teaching teens. They are often broken down into "small groups" where the teen's opinion is solicited about how they 'feel' about the teaching of the Church. This only encourages the "Religion of Self" within the Faith as it fosters a delusion that the teen's opinion actually matters to the Reality of the universe. Furthermore, there is inconsistency with what is being taught about the Faith. And frankly, some of these volunteers, God bless them and their willingness to serve, are not very good at it. I found that a good teacher is as effective teaching 10 teens as that same teacher would be teaching 1000. Why would we not allow our youth to be taught by the very best teachers of our Faith? Why not have those who teach youth for a living and are comfortable with it, teach the masses. Camp Veritas could then be the one place a parish would know their kids are being taught by the best teachers that the Catholic Church has to offer and taught the Faith consistent with our teaching authority of Rome.

Camp Veritas would teach the kids how to pray. Most simply do not know how. They have never been exposed to prayer. Camp would fill them with grace through Confession and the reception of the Eucharist, and introduce them to a vibrant community of believers, including priests and other religious.

The key to this experience is to introduce the teens to the Lord at a rate that is tolerable. Pouring knowledge of the Truth onto a teen when their glass is already overflowing is not useful or fun. The average human being has about 45 min of attention before they cannot compute any more information at that time. The key to this challenge is great entertainment in between the religious instruction so the teens do not feel like they are in class all day. This allows the teaching moments to soak in. This means Camp Veritas could be held anywhere the teens can eat, sleep, be taught, and entertained for a week. In short, the objective of the week would be to play and pray and activate in each young Catholic camper the following desire: to reevaluate their life priorities by questioning where they came from and where they are going, and continue *in the Lord* one step at a time up the mountain of life.

My initial approach was to propose the idea to the staff of the Archdiocese of New York. The response I got from them was essentially, "Great, we'll pray for YOU in this mission!" My reaction was human and typical. I thought they didn't understand that I was trying to have them focus *their* resources on the youth in this venture. The next step was to send another letter, only this time directly to Cardinal Egan—the man at the top at the time—reiterating the concept of Camp Veritas. Much to my disappointment, the response from him was essentially the same. This time, Cardinal Egan himself wrote me a letter again essentially stating, "Good luck. I will pray for YOU." My reaction was, "great, now what? What do I know about leading a camp? What do I know about leading youth? Who would come to a camp run by the random guy named Ryan Young anyway? What kind of credibility do I have? Where, in all my education regarding medicine, have I ever been taught these skills? I did not even go to camp as a kid. Has the Lord lost His mind?"

Also, it quickly became apparent to me that starting a camp would entail a lot of time and money. It would detract from my family responsibilities. I was being called into a service that would entail a great sacrifice of my time which would challenge my call as husband and father. Like any man who goes to war, I was a man being called into the battle of souls. **I had to be willing to sacrifice the time I might spend with my family so at some point, my children can live in a much better world.**

My saving grace is that my wife has always been onboard. She has the same priorities in her life that I have in mine. Our priority is Heaven. It is through this reality that she feels called to "hold down the fort". Her attitude allows me to then "go forth." I have been truly blessed to have a wife that understands the big picture; she is like the supply train to the battlefield for souls.

The Lord was showing me the first few steps of the "mountain in the fog," so I started climbing. After all, if *I* do not act, who will? I started this climb up this mountain with the foundation of who I am; I began by presenting the idea of Camp Veritas to my immediate family. After all, they are the most Catholic people I know. These are God's saints. My family is full of holy, talented, and intelligent people who love the Church. They are not blind to the bleak future of our Church in our region if nothing changes. The reaction I received from those I love most was surprising. My parents and most my siblings shook their heads and laughed and told me that an idea of this magnitude could not be done. I was told it was "unrealistic" and the problems we face in our Church were simply "too big."

My older brother, who has been a great example of faith to me in my life, relayed his personal experience with trying to renew our Faith. A year earlier, he tried to start a prayer group for his parish. He invited hundreds of young adults to his parish for their opening meeting. Flyers were placed at numerous local parishes. My brother wanted to order fifteen pizzas for the crowd he was expecting. To his dismay, his parish priest ordered three pizzas and told my brother he would order more if needed. Needless to say, 3 people showed up. Those three people were himself and his brother and sister. My brother's conclusion was that the Church was already dead in our region and beyond life-support.

My older sister whose conversion was the catalyst of my family's conversion in the Faith, who attends daily mass and home-schools her eight saintly children, did not believe teenagers would ever willingly attend this camp, much less convince their parents to pay a fee for them to attend. She brought up the numerous logistical challenges I would face in opening a camp, such as adult volunteer supervision, need for lifeguards, entertainment, and so forth. As she spoke, the mountain of this task the Lord placed in front of me was unveiled. This mountain was enormous. The journey ahead seemed hard, practically impossible. That moment reminds me of when Peter tried to convince Jesus not to enter Jerusalem where He would be crucified and "At this he turned around and, looking at his disciples, rebuked Peter and said, 'Get behind me Satan. You are thinking not as God does, but as human beings do.'"(Mk 8:33)

My younger sister is one of the most holy people I know. She spends over an hour each day in Eucharistic Adoration. Not only did she think the idea of this Camp was too big; she especially thought the idea was too big for me. The problem I was facing with my family is that they know me the most. They know of my many weaknesses. They know the road I have traveled. She had no faith in *me*. What she didn't realize is that I do not have faith in *me* either. I am nothing in the grand scheme of things. Who am I to even attempt something as crazy as Camp Veritas? She believed I was having delusions of grandeur. Although I don't believe I am a prophet, it reminds me of Jesus saying, "Amen, I say to you, no prophet is accepted in his own native place."(Lk 4:24) My immediate family, who is religious, did not believe in this idea. Considering the poor state the Church is in, what would the rest of the Church family think?

Ironically, the only person in my immediate family who thought the idea of Camp Veritas had any value and didn't shoot the idea down outright was my youngest sister (the same sister who finally attended Mass after the fly repeated landed on her face.) Go figure?

The truth is that my family was right. All of their objections and concerns were completely valid. I did not have any answers for them. In fact, I agreed with all of their objections. I thought the Lord was crazy for asking me to start a camp. But that was the point. The only thing I really knew for certain was that the Lord was asking me to do this. I had faith in that call of the heart. I had faith without understanding. Although I felt completely alone at that moment, although the mountain looked too big for me to climb, the only response I could give to my family was, "**I told the Lord I would try to answer His call and that I would give my absolute best, so I intend on doing so.**"

The next few steps of the "mountain in the fog" emerged and I climbed further. I spent most of my "free time" for a year getting the camp off the ground. I was forced to do things like call strangers. As an introvert, I would first develop a cold sweat and get nauseated as I paced around the phone. Then I would say to myself, "For your Glory Lord," pick up the phone and dial before I could change my mind. I would make a call to someone I thought could help, and they would advise me to call someone else to cover other aspects of logistics and so forth. The Holy Spirit took me step by step because I had no idea what I was doing. I was a man on a mission and I would not take "no" for an answer. "**No**" **was not a possibility to me. I was on a mission from God. The only thing that mattered was how I was to get to "yes."** Ultimately, after a year's worth of efforts and promotion, and with the help of my father behind the scenes, handling all of the processes of a corporation, the pieces of Camp Veritas quickly fell into place and the Camp was ready to receive camper enrollments.

I have generally been successful in my worldly endeavors throughout my whole life. I have always done well in school, work, finances and so forth. I 'succeeded' at most things I attempted. With regards to the camp, the number of enrollments compared to my expectations was pathetic. We were not even close to reaching the minimum number of campers that we had negotiated in our contract with the camp facility we planned to rent for the week. This was like the prayer-group pizza party my brother had thrown for his parish, however multiplying that disaster times 100. I felt like the Ark had been built, it was raining heavily, but nobody was getting into the boat. I was embarrassed for our Church. I really did not know how to explain to the camp facility how the entire Catholic Church in our region only had about 12 teens willing to come. Frankly, it was a really distressing time.

In the worldly sense, I had failed. I had tried my very best and I had failed. I was ready to give up and cancel the project. It was at this moment of decision, lying in bed late one night, that I prayed to God in relative despair. Much to my surprise and relief, thoughts from the Lord suddenly flowed through my mind. He made me aware that it was not *my* money I had spent on camp, nor *my* time. In fact, Camp Veritas was not *my* camp at all. The Lord reminded me that I had already given Him everything that I am. My life is His. It was therefore *His* money, *His* time, *His* camp. **There was also no such thing as failure in attempting to do the will of the Lord because, in obeying Him—in taking those steps up that mountain—I have already won.** God never guaranteed *worldly* success. He did, however, promise to provide me with peace and joy if I obeyed, and ultimately, on that front, He came through.

He then gave me a more dramatic vision. The Camp Veritas paradigm would ultimately exist in every diocese of the country as a "boot camp for souls." Our youth would all attend camp as the norm for their Catholic upbringing in their immediate pre and post Confirmation time. They would take spiritual tools from camp that could be applied in their home, their church, and their community for years to come. They would take the spiritual fire they received from the camp and use it to expel the darkness they encountered in our culture. They would participate in the transfiguration of the "Mystical Body of Christ." They would participate in the revolution against the "Religion of Self."

As I saw this vision in my mind, I literally laughed out loud. The thought of national expansion was a ridiculous thought when only a dozen teens signed up after a year of effort. I felt like the elderly, childless Sarah when God assured her husband Abraham that "you will have descendants as numerous as the stars."(Gen22:17) I brashly told God that He had better get cracking given that our Camp Veritas situation did not look very good. The next day, I met with my local bishop and he encouraged me to persist, so I went back to my journey and took another step up the mountain.

Ultimately, many members of my family got on board with the idea of Camp Veritas and started to help out. With their efforts, over 50 youth attended the first year. The recipe of Camp Veritas was now tested and perfected. We were delighted that the kids got so much out of it. Prior to our first camp, I received a warning call from a mother telling me she was sending her very resistant 17 year old son to camp. On the last day of camp this same teen said, "You saved a lot of souls this week, including my own." Two years later, as Cardinal Timothy Dolan's van drove into camp, that same former camper jumped out of the van as a seminarian.

Meeting Cardinal Dolan at Camp Veritas was somewhat surreal. As I gave him a tour of the facility, I told him of the vision of "franchising" the Camp Veritas recipe and taking it everywhere. If it worked in New York, why would the same recipe not work in Chicago, Los Angeles, Denver, Miami, St. Louis, or Seattle? Unlike so many times before with so many other people, he listened and did not look at me like I was totally crazy. After he heard the plan, he looked at me with a wry smile as stated, "How far are you willing to go?" I answered, "How much is a soul worth?" Every day, as I awake to this battle for souls, those words ring out to me, "**How far are you willing to go, Ryan? How much is a soul worth?**"

As I have had the honor of getting to know Cardinal Dolan a bit over the past year, and after seeing how filled he is with the Holy Spirit, I am no longer laughing incredulously at God any longer. With his help and with the help of my family and many others, Camp Veritas is expanding rapidly. We are approaching our fifth year and now have 450 enrollments from 10 states divided into 2 camps with over 100 support staff, yet this is still just the beginning.

I learned through this experience to be at peace with God's plan and give up control. I learned that the Lord will use me in ways I would not have expected. I learned not to put limits on the Lord and to stop guessing how long and difficult the journey will be up the mountain of my life. I learned to have faith and trust in the Lord. I learned how to properly measure success in my life. **I learned that nothing is impossible with God!**

The Camp Veritas portion of my journey up the mountain of life continues for me, my family, the campers, the adult volunteers, the dedicated priests, religious sisters and friars, and the camper's parents. If you have an interest in learning more about the camp—the boot camp for souls—please check us out at www.campveritas.com.

IF I WERE SATAN

I GREW UP PLAYING CHESS. The key to playing chess well is to anticipate your opponent's next move and act accordingly. I have a singular remaining mission in my life: That is to bring as many eternal souls that I possibly can to the foot of the Cross and allow the Lord to do the rest. That mission has become an obsession of sorts. I have found that it influences every decision I make every day. It is the reason I am writing this book, at this very moment.

Satan also has a singular objective. His only mission is to draw us away from the Cross. He uses the dust of the world to do so. He is a cunning adversary and the moment we let up our guard to him is the moment he has already won.

The following thoughts are my thoughts. These thoughts are simply what I would do if I were Satan. These are not necessarily the teaching of the Catholic Church.

As I have already died to myself, I have nothing left to lose. What is Satan going to do to me? Kill me twice? With that freedom, I have been able to run about the battlefield and assess the situation. Right now, it is like Satan is on a hill, lobbing mortar fire on our entrenched positions. We, the Church, have been hiding defensively in our bunkers for decades, hoping he won't aim at us next. For many, the bunkers have become entirely too comfortable. Slowly but surely, Satan is taking out our positions, one school, one hospital, and one church at a time.

He has amassed an army that is presently on the move at high speed due to our new digital age. As he seems to be working through the internet, the Catholic Church still seems to be using the pony express. Satan is succeeding because of several tactics. First, as already discussed throughout this book, corrupt the souls of all through the "Religion of

Self." Next, if I were Satan, I would control information. Control TV, the radio, movies, education, and print literature. Frame all Truth in his agenda, twisting that Truth slowly enough that from moment to moment, we are unaware of how far we have turned from the Lord.

Recently, after flipping through 200 channels, my wife stated, "Where have all of the men gone?" The guys on TV are either stupid, act like a bunch of pre-pubescent boys or college partying idiots, or are prancing around the TV as if they are women. When is the last time you have seen a strong, upright, confident man sacrificing himself for anything other than self on TV? The last time I can remember seeing a normal, traditional family on TV was the Cosby Show, Little House on the Prairie, or Family Ties in the 1980's. There is EWTN, the Catholic channel. It is nicely tucked away on channel 97 within an ocean of other channels. Out of sight, out of mind.

Who is Catholic on TV that accurately teaches or stands for the teaching of our Catholic Church? Bishop Fulton Sheen used to be that face in the 1950's. Now, the only 'Catholics' we are exposed to publically are those that are in blatant opposition and even scandal against the Church, especially regarding issues of life. These include Lawrence O'donnell and Chris Mathews on MSNBC or leading politicians with great influence like Nancy Pelosi, Joe Biden, John Kerry, Andrew Cuomo, and Rudy Giuliani. If I were Satan, I would encourage that "scandal" (open opposition to the Catholic Church while proclaiming to be a Catholic themselves) to run amuck so to be "Catholic" really doesn't mean anything because all the "Catholics" we ever publically see seem to believe in what they please, not serving a Truth larger than themself. They clearly seem to value their political worldly success and affiliation more than their identity as Catholic.

If I were Satan, and I wanted to control information, I would control schools. I would put an emphasis on the good of public education in a community; such an emphasis that the populous would feel compelled through misdirected compassion to *pay anything* for it. The disproportionate cost of public schools would then create a tax culture where although we are "free" to have a Catholic education, after paying our public school taxes, nobody can afford to go to a catholic school. After a while, I would make it illegal to home-school children, as of course the government could educate our kids better than our parents can, so it would be child-abuse to not put our children in public school, right?

If I were Satan, I would emphasize the beauty of God's creation of our planet and environment so much, that it would encourage people to fall in love with creation rather than the Creator. I would create a culture where having children would actually be viewed as selfish, as children might require resources and might therefore be harmful to "mother earth" so out of compassion to mother earth, laws would be construed to limit the number of children we have. China's present 1 child only per family while the rest are slaughtered through abortion would be the next logical step.

If I were Satan, I would slowly force the populous to participate in sin. This would foster an attitude where because we are already forced to sin, what is just one more? We already pay for abortion as tax payers in this country indirectly. We subsidize Planned Parenthood with our tax dollars which pays for the building where abortions are performed, the abortion "doctor's" salaries, the heat, overhead, and equipment. If that is the case, out of "compassion" for "woman's health," why not force Catholic institutions and employers to directly pay for early abortion-causing drugs for their staff? Note that the media intentionally and repeatedly calls these drugs "contraception," not the "morning after pills" that many of these truly represent.

If I were Satan, I would attack the Catholic Church's freedom of speech. I would make sin legal, like "gay marriage," so if the Church was to speak out against this *sin*, it would be construed as "hate speech," discrimination, or bigotry. Right now in England, yes I did not say Syria or China, I said England; a woman lost her job because she wore a small cross to work. If I were Satan, I would classify all discussion about faith, the "imposing" of religion on others and eventually remove all discussion about God from everywhere unless one wanted to risk fines or imprisonment. This, of course would be out of "compassion" for unbelievers.

If I were Satan, I would encourage dependence of a populace on government, not God. For millennia, the Catholic Church has been the staple in culture to serve and educate the poor and the infirmed. The

Church was able to freely contribute its 2000 years of knowledge and wisdom through its service to society. The Catholic Church *invented* the University, the Hospital, and organized charity. This was supported financially through the *voluntary* charity of those in the pew, the "Body of Christ."

If I were Satan, I would use our rightful compassion to the infirmed, the aged, children, and the handicap and then push to extend that compassion to the 'takers' of our society. Working in health care, I am exposed daily to those who are completely able-bodied, taking advantage of the *forced* charity of others through governmental subsidy. I deal with numerous "disabled" people who can still drive, talk, walk, and go bowling. It is not that these individuals can't work, they simply choose not to. Through "Misdirected Compassion," they take from the government free education, housing, food, health care, transportation, cable television, air-conditioning, retirement, and a cell phone. Why work? The amount of 'takers' has become an epidemic. I am often exposed to people who seem to have enough money for expensive hair styling, designer clothing, manicures, and cigarettes yet these same individuals claim they do not have enough money for the $10 copay of their own child's medicine.

Forced charity (another term for slavery) through tax, removes all grace from charity. By forcefully taking money from those who are working, because that person did not freely give that money away, he does not receive grace. He does not take any step toward the objective of Heaven. Those who are taking that money to remain "disabled," or purposely unemployed, grow in a sense of entitlement, not gratitude, and therefore the recipient of those funds does not receive grace either. "When we were with you, we instructed you that if anyone was unwilling to work, neither should that one eat."(2Th3:10). Christ did not tell his apostles to *force* the rich man to give away his goods to the poor. Christ *invites us* to make that choice.

A Catholic is to fight that everybody in a society has the *opportunity*, the *freedom*, to make good choices and have the ability to labor for a just wage. A Catholic is not obligated to perpetually enable sloth and dependence. A Catholic is not obligated to perpetually bail out those making bad decisions. God, through love, has given us the ability to make decisions, some good and some bad. He allows us to experience the consequences of those decisions, good and bad. In other words, if a Catholic truly loves his brother, instead of fostering dependence by perpetually giving the "hungry" fish, the Catholic would instead teach the hungry to fish themselves, fostering freedom from dependence.

A Catholic would also care for those who are vulnerable, those who have no ability to physically contribute to the community such as the very old, very young, mentally handicapped, or the very sick as we understand the value of human dignity because the breath of God is in them.

If I were Satan, I would encourage economic dependence on government, removing the freedom of a populace to exercise free-will, creating a form of slavery. Just ask anyone who has fled Russia, East Berlin, North Korea, and China how the government ultimately becomes the people's 'god.' Ask then how free they were to believe in the true God of the Universe. Ask how free the Catholic Church was in serving the community in those countries. Can you think of one Socialistic or Communist Country where the Catholic Church is presently growing? A government that wants to be 'god' usually does not like competitors.

If I were Satan, I would do everything I could to promote Islamic violent extremism. Pope Benedict the XVI was right when he noted, "How true can a faith be if one needs a gun to promote it?" As the world goes to war with Islamic violent extremism, is it so hard to imagine this war of violence spreading onto religion itself, including Christianity? Satan does not care about politics. He does not care about maps. He cares only for souls.

If I was Satan, I would attack the priesthood with everything I got. Take down the shepherd, you scatter the sheep. I would dig up every scandal I possibly could in the Church over the past 50 years. Every time the Catholic Church is discussed, I would somehow incorporate the word "scandal" in the same article. I would want to destroy the credibility of the Church to the population it serves.

If I were Satan, I would cause as much division as I could within the Church itself. I would encourage, through pride, many religious to disregard their authority in Rome. I would encourage "pluralism" and "tolerance" to the point where heresy would be accepted as merely another point of view; where there was no longer a memory of the objective Truth of Jesus Christ or his teaching authority in the Magisterium.

If I were Satan, I would paint the Catholic Church as a non-compassionate, scandal ridden entity of old men who are out of date with an "enlightened" world. I would paint the Catholic Church as sexist, bigoted, intolerant, and did I already mention, non-compassionate? Do not the points of this chapter seem familiar to us all? Have we not all seen this organized, systematic attack from Satan spreading throughout our land like a tsunami that is wiping out all that is good? How long are we going to stay down, hiding in our bunker? *How many souls are we willing to lose* while we wait around, hoping that some other person acts as Christ's voice, hands, and feet?!

No more . . . NO MORE!! It is time to charge the hill! I have breath right now. You have breath right now. If we do not act, who will? If now is not the time to act, then when? Once there is no one left? In Christ, *we* are the hope of the future in this world! We have the opportunity to face these forces of darkness head on. The Truth of our Faith should never be in retreat. We should never operate in fear! **One hour of Truth dispels years of lies.** Even the smallest light in Truth is bright in the darkness. We should never go away! We should never go quietly into the night! We are Disciples of Jesus Christ that need to stand as one and charge Satan's position on that hill together. In doing so, we can and will win this war for souls. Christ, through the Cross has already given us the victory! We now, through our voices and talents in love, have the opportunity to bring this victory to the world as the "Good News." We must bring to all people of the world the light of His victory! **How far are you willing to go? How much is a soul worth? Answer the call! Answer the call! And together in Christ, we will change the world!!**

DISCIPLESHIP

ALL RIGHT RYAN. I JUST finished reading the last chapter. Although I think you should consider taking some valium, I am inspired to go out and save the world from itself! Now what? . . . **BE YOURSELF!** God has made you a unique, one of a kind, masterpiece! There has never been, nor will there ever be, anyone in the history of world just like you. God made you with specific talents and unique abilities. All He asks of us is that we offer the only thing we have the power to offer; to give our will to Him. In giving Him our will, we are giving Him our talents and gifts and ultimately our lives.

When I started to journey with the Lord up this 'mountain of fog' in faith, I had some fear. One of my greatest fears was that in giving my will to the Lord, He might call me to be a hermit wearing a loin cloth in the desert of Africa. In giving up control of my life to Him and in dying to myself, becoming a hermit might actually be a possibility. What I have found is that if I am to truly give up control to Him, another possibility is that the Lord may decide He would like me to be a steward of worldly wealth and may have me become financially "successful." What I am discovering through prayer and experience is that the wealth I have in my soul has very little to do with the monetary wealth I have. That is why one might find as many millionaires who are completely miserable as poor people who are blissfully joyful. In short, money has everything to do with temporal 'happiness' and very little to do with lasting 'joy.'

It reminds me of a scene in a movie called "Ironman" (2008). There is this billionaire character, who is all alone in his life, and who is captured by terrorists and thrown into a prison cell. In the cell with him is a poor gentleman who has a loving family which he longs to rejoin. After sharing their respective stories, the poor man ultimately tells the billionaire, "You have everything, yet you have nothing." How true that statement is for so many people across the financial spectrum.

Now it turns out that when we look at the lives of the saints, some of them were, in fact, financially wealthy kings or popes, yet many were poor like St. Francis. In the end, *the attachment* to worldly goods is what it is we must avoid. A saint can live the life set forth by God in peace and joy, using the 'stuff' God chooses to give to him or not. The saint should always be ready to give back the Lord's "stuff" to Him when He asks for it. That is the moment of truth experienced by the "rich man" in Scripture who was unwilling to "sell all he had and follow the Lord." That is why for most, "it is easier for a camel to pass through the eye of a needle than for a rich man to enter the Kingdom of Heaven." (Mt19:24)

With monetary wealth, it is also easy to forget whose 'stuff' it is. Being a god unto oneself and forgetting that "There is a God and I am not Him" is much easier if the person is financially wealthy. It is easier for the wealthy to forget that they are dust, and that their ultimate purpose is to know and serve the Lord. It is easier to become spiritually apathetic about their dependence on God when they have no material needs. The Truth is that one does not really need much material stuff beyond the basics of life: food and basic housing. Beyond those basics, money has very little to do with lasting peace and joy. All the poor owns is their trust in the Lord. With that simplicity comes much peace.

In trying to discern what God wanted me to do with my life, I needed to first identify *who I am*. Most people of the world identify themselves as what they do or what they are good at. I used to be just a student, a musician, an athlete, a member of my family. Then at some point, my most basic identity dawned on me. **Through my baptism, I am a Prince. I am Heir to the Kingdom of Heaven. I am a disciple of Jesus Christ.** Nothing else I do in this world is more important than that reality. When the world identifies me as crazy or "unenlightened," I answer, "Perhaps, but I am a Prince and Heir to the Kingdom of Heaven. I am a disciple of Jesus Christ so who cares how *you* want to identify me?" **I know who I am.**

I am no longer defined by the world. God Himself paid the price at the Cross *for me*. It is He who identifies me as one of His children. It is He that established my value. Through my new identity in Christ, it is not like I am just hanging around, expecting God to rain manna down from the sky on me or something. I have taken my true identity in Christ and super infused that identity on the rest of my being. With that new identity, I live what most would classify as a very ordinary life. I still do everything I used to do, I just do it for a different reason. Within the identity of Christ however, my life is anything but ordinary. I have purpose and meaning, even while just doing the dishes. I have joy, even when just cutting the lawn. I have peace in the simple things: a sunset, watching the kids play and laugh, hearing the cows' next door moo, feeling the breeze on my face, listening to the rain. My identity in Him has changed everything about me.

In giving up our lives to Him and allowing Him to be our Master, there is peace and joy in everything we do. Although our lives may seem very 'ordinary' to most, when we are living our lives for the Lord, whether we are teachers or housekeepers or doctors, there is nothing 'ordinary' about our lives. We have purpose. We have reason for our being. We have life. We have freedom.

What the Lord asks of me is that I use the talents and gifts He gave me for *His* glory, not for mine. He built me with the intelligence and personality to work in health care, so I am a Physician Assistant for His glory. He has called me to be a husband and father. I have therefore been married for fourteen years and have five children for His glory. He has given me the talent of singing; I therefore cantor at my church for His glory. He has given me the ability to speak; I therefore minister to all who are open to hearing the Truth, and many who are not. He has given me the ability to teach; I am therefore writing this book. I must always remind myself that in all that I do, in all that I achieve, I am nothing but dust, as are my 'accomplishments.' The major difference with my new identity in Christ is my choice to now live for God's glory and not for my own.

God has given each of us a myriad of talents and abilities. He will use us uniquely as we are created uniquely. The "Body of Christ" has many parts. Although the parts are different, they are all special and important. My path up the mountain is likely to be somewhat different than yours because we are different parts of this one, living body. We are uniquely made. We are the salt of the Earth! (Mt 5:13)

God has built some of us to be professional athletes, so be the best athlete you can be for the glory of God. He has built others to stay at home and raise children; so raise the greatest, holiest children for the glory of God. He has built others to be investment bankers; so be a great banker for the glory of God. God has built others to be garbage collectors; so be the best garbage collector this world has ever seen for His glory. God has built others to become priests; thank you Lord for these holy men. No matter what our talents, no matter what our station in life or how much money we have, we have the chance to stand out as an example to others and give God glory. Wherever this journey with the Lord leads us, we have a chance to be a light in the darkness.

God has a plan for you. Isn't that a cool thought? God has an adventure in store *for you* from this point forward, an adventure that will have you climbing higher on the 'mountain of life' than you had ever dreamed possible. He has an adventure planned for you whereby He will expand the capacity of your very being in every aspect of your life. He is calling *you* to shine like the sun. He is ready to tap *your* incredible potential. *You* are called to be the greatest saint this world has ever seen. Find your identity in Christ! Walk with the Lord on this journey! Never stray from His side! Never lose hope! Never forget about the finish line!

I pray that the Lord will mold us into His image. I pray for the grace to do His will. I pray that we will all have the courage to reach up and take His hand and allow Him to lead us in this first step up our personal mountain of life to His Glory forever and ever! Amen.

Epilogue

To my children:

Kids, I am so sorry that at times during this mission for the Lord, I did not have as much time and attention to give you that I would have wanted. I just want you each to know that you were all on my mind and heart, every moment of the days that I was not able to be with you. I hope that through the sacrifice of my time away from you that I helped make a planet that was easier for you to be in relationship with God. I look forward to spending eternity with each of you in the paradise of Heaven. I am so very proud of all of you. I am *honored* to have had the privilege to be your father. I love you all.

CPSIA information can be obtained at www.ICGtesting.com
Printed in the USA
BVOW021921260712

296285BV00001B/3/P